AVALON CASTLE

Built by Ambrose Blackwood, an eccentric obsessed by the legend of King Arthur, Avalon Castle is a disturbing place housing very dark secrets. When Rachel Garland visits in 1867, she hopes to spend a peaceful Christmas with her half-sister Lucy. But what she finds is a house filled with rumoured hauntings, family feuds, and unnerving disappearances. Then the festive mood is destroyed by a death, and Rachel's discomfort grows as her questions mount. With the help of William Norton, a neighbouring landowner, she searches for evidence to prove her suspicions of foul play — but her investigations will lead her into deadly peril . . .

Books by Rosemary Craddock
Published by Ulverscroft:

THE LOVEGROVE HERMIT

SPECIAL MESSAGE TO READERS

THE ULVERSCROFT FOUNDATION
(registered UK charity number 264873)
was established in 1972 to provide funds for
research, diagnosis and treatment of eye diseases.
Examples of major projects funded by
the Ulverscroft Foundation are:-

- The Children's Eye Unit at Moorfields Eye Hospital, London
- The Ulverscroft Children's Eye Unit at Great Ormond Street Hospital for Sick Children
- Funding research into eye diseases and treatment at the Department of Ophthalmology, University of Leicester
- The Ulverscroft Vision Research Group, Institute of Child Health
- Twin operating theatres at the Western Ophthalmic Hospital, London
- The Chair of Ophthalmology at the Royal Australian College of Ophthalmologists

You can help further the work of the Foundation
by making a donation or leaving a legacy.
Every contribution is gratefully received. If you
would like to help support the Foundation or
require further information, please contact:

THE ULVERSCROFT FOUNDATION
**The Green, Bradgate Road, Anstey
Leicester LE7 7FU, England
Tel: (0116) 236 4325**

website: www.foundation.ulverscroft.com

Rosemary Craddock was born in Staffordshire and has lived there most of her life. She has been writing since childhood and has published many novels full of mystery, romance and intrigue, most of them set in the nineteenth century.

ROSEMARY CRADDOCK

◆

AVALON CASTLE

Complete and Unabridged

ULVERSCROFT
Leicester

First published in Great Britain in 2015 by
Robert Hale Limited
London

First Large Print Edition
published 2016
by arrangement with
Robert Hale
an imprint of The Crowood Press
Wiltshire

A catalogue record for this book is available
from the British Library.

ISBN 978–1–4448–3046–0

Published by
F. A. Thorpe (Publishing)
Anstey, Leicestershire

Set by Words & Graphics Ltd.
Anstey, Leicestershire
Printed and bound in Great Britain by
T. J. International Ltd., Padstow, Cornwall

The Passing of Arthur

I am going a long way [. . .]
To the island-valley of Avilion;
Where falls not hail, or rain, or any snow,
Nor ever wind blows loudly; but it lies
Deep-meadow'd, happy, fair with
orchard-lawns
And bowery hollows crown'd with
summer sea [. . .]

Alfred, Lord Tennyson

1

'Look, Rachel, there's Mr Rochester again. You know, I think he's rather interested in us. He always seems to be wandering in our direction and he stares quite rudely. Perhaps you have an admirer.'

'Gentlemen are not in the habit of staring at me,' I said, 'and certainly not when you are here. Anyway, I never did find Mr Rochester very fascinating, so I give him to you with pleasure.'

My sister Lucy and I sat on the beach every day when the weather was fine and we had given nicknames to all the people we saw regularly. There was the Wan Widow, pale-faced in her black crape, attended by her hobbledehoy son. There was the Pickle family: a crowd of noisy, adventurous children who were always falling off donkeys or into the sea. There were the Honeymooners, who sat holding hands and never spoke. And there was Mr Rochester.

It was inevitable that the dark, heavily built man with his strong, harsh features and air of brooding melancholy should be Mr Rochester. *Jane Eyre* was Lucy's favourite novel.

'He's really rather intriguing,' said Lucy, peeping under the brim of her straw hat so that she could inspect the stranger without his being aware of it. 'He's always on his own and looks so unhappy. A lonely widower, do you think?'

'If so, perhaps we can match him up with the Wan Widow.'

'I wonder who he is?'

'That we'll never know,' I said lightly. But I was wrong.

My half-sister Lucy was my junior by nine years and so different in appearance that no one would suppose we were related at all. I was thirty and considered myself rather plain. My father always told me I had beautiful eyes — a compliment commonly paid to women who have nothing else to praise. They were undoubtedly my best feature as they were large and bright, but they did little to compensate for straight mousy hair, a long nose and a wide mouth. Lucy, in contrast, was a beauty.

Ill health, which Lucy had suffered since an attack of rheumatic fever at fifteen, often ruins a woman's looks but it had merely given Lucy an air of fragility. She was delicately fair, with a pale complexion, blue eyes and an enchantingly pretty face.

Since our father's death two years ago we

had lived in Northgate on the coast of Kent. As Papa had been a clergyman we had been obliged to leave the comfortable rectory where we had been brought up and so decided on a seaside resort as the air had been recommended for Lucy's health. There were other reasons. The town was cheerful and busy so my sister could have rest and diversion. Here she could take gentle walks, go for drives, visit the circulating library, attend concerts, dine with some of the friends we had made, or simply sit on the beach and be entertained by her surroundings.

That golden September afternoon a minor accident pitched us both into a different world. The misadventure was the work of the Pickle family. Two of the boys, kicking a ball about, sent it flying in our direction and it caught Lucy on the side of the head so that she was thrown to the ground.

We were soon surrounded by a crowd of well-meaning people, offering help and advice, holding out brandy flasks and smelling salts. I leaned over my sister, calling her name. Her eyes were open but she looked bewildered; she groaned a little and put up her hand to her head.

'Will you all stand back, please; the young lady needs air,' said a deep, authoritative voice as Mr Rochester took command. He felt Lucy's pulse and then helped her to sit up, taking the Wan Widow's smelling salts and holding them briefly below Lucy's nose. He then unceremoniously removed her hat and felt her head.

'No great harm done, fortunately,' he said.

'Excuse me, sir, are you a doctor?' I enquired.

'No, but I'm not entirely lacking in either common knowledge or common sense. As for you,' he turned suddenly on the two Pickle boys who were hovering anxiously nearby, 'if you want to kill anyone, don't do it here. Find something useful to occupy your idle hours.'

'But, sir, we're very sorry. We didn't mean any harm, we didn't think — '

'You didn't think, I'm sure,' said Mr Rochester with heavy irony and the culprits crept away.

By now Lucy was herself again, although she complained of feeling a little dizzy. Our new acquaintance enquired where we lived and offered to accompany us home.

'If you are climbing the cliff path the young lady will need help,' he informed me. 'If necessary I will carry her.'

'That is very kind of you, sir, but we — '

'It's settled, then. Come along, gather your belongings.' He helped Lucy to her feet.

I was not used to dealing with overbearing

and presumptuous men. Papa had been the soul of courtesy and gentleness and I was not too pleased by the stranger's peremptory manner.

'We are very much obliged to you, sir, but we don't know you,' I said, having concluded that brusqueness was best countered with absolute candour.

'That's soon remedied. My name is Blackwood — Nicholas Blackwood. I am staying at the Belle Vue Hotel and I can provide you with a full biography if so desired, but at present I think we should concentrate on removing your friend to a quiet spot where she can recover.'

As he had introduced himself I saw nothing for it but to tell him our names, and soon we were making our way up the cliff path, Mr Blackwood supporting Lucy, followed by me with the rugs, cushions and novels.

Although I was uneasy about a strange man taking over I reflected that he had an educated voice, though with a slight, indefinable accent, and dressed like a gentleman. In any case we would soon be rid of him. When we reached The Laurels he took his leave of us, expressing the hope that we might meet again in the not too distant future.

'In more agreeable circumstances perhaps,'

he added, and then smiled for the first time.

As graciously as I could I thanked him for his help and bade him goodbye. Lucy extended her hand and murmured a few words of gratitude before he turned to go. Once inside the house Lucy's old nurse Mattie came bustling to help and my sister was soon lying on the sofa, being plied with every kind of restorative.

'I really am very much better,' she protested at last. 'I wasn't hurt at all.'

'There is a bruise appearing,' said Mattie, applying arnica.

'What does that matter? Oh, Rachel, what did you think of Mr Rochester coming to our aid? We really ought to write and thank him.'

I hesitated. 'I'm not sure that is necessary. We thanked him verbally and he only did what any gentleman might do in the circumstances. He was not greatly inconvenienced.'

Perhaps, at the back of my mind, was a faint tremor of unease — that instinct which tells me, on first meeting a person, whether there is something of which one should be wary.

'I think it would be very rude *not* to write and if you don't, I shall!' declared Lucy stubbornly.

There was no arguing with Lucy once she

made up her mind; for all her fragile looks she had a determination and an obstinacy that were difficult to thwart. Perhaps the combination of beauty and delicate health had led to her being overindulged and as I was among those who had helped to spoil her I could scarcely complain at the result.

'We'll see,' I said soothingly, 'but now you'd better rest for a while. Your health is more important than Mr Rochester.'

2

It was a week before we resumed our visits to the beach. Our absence was occasioned more by an abrupt change in the weather than by Lucy's indisposition, which had proved trifling. When we were once more favoured with a beautiful day we returned to our usual place. There were considerably fewer people about. The Wan Widow and the Honeymooners had departed and the mother of the Pickles, who came over to enquire after Lucy's health, informed us they were leaving at the end of the week.

'The season is almost over,' I said to Lucy. I did wonder, briefly, if Mr Blackwood had gone too. 'We'd better make the most of what is left,' I observed, 'because there may not be many more days of sitting on the beach.'

I was aware of the crunching of steps on the shingle but took little notice until they stopped behind us and a deep voice spoke. It was Mr Blackwood.

'Miss Garland — Miss Lucy Garland — I am glad to see you about again, looking so well. It was kind of you to write but my attentions were so slight that it was not necessary to thank me.'

I raised an eyebrow at my sister. She had not said any more about writing to her rescuer and she had the grace to colour.

It was impossible now to avoid his company. He carried a plaid rug over his arm and, after asking if he might join us, he spread it on the pebbles beside me and sat down. He proved to be by no means a disagreeable companion. Although his occupation seemed to be a family business in Birmingham he had travelled in France and Germany and once, during the late Civil War, to America. He had read widely and met a variety of people, so his conversation was interesting. My initial feeling of annoyance wore off and soon we were all chatting like old friends. He told us of his family; he had a brother and sister, both unmarried, who lived in Worcestershire.

'I join them at weekends, or whenever I can spare a day or two away from my work. I live in Birmingham most of the time.'

'Then you have no family of your own?' asked Lucy with an interested look.

'My wife died two years ago. I have an eight-year-old daughter but she lives at Kilwood with my brother and sister.'

'Oh, poor child!' exclaimed Lucy. 'I lost my mother when I was five but of course I had dear Rachel, who was almost like a second mother to me.'

'Ah, yes.' He favoured me with one of his rare smiles. 'I am sure she has fulfilled that duty with great affection and devotion.'

During the next few days we were gradually drawn into a friendship with Mr Blackwood. He joined us on the beach; he invited us to accompany him to a concert in the Assembly Rooms; he bought us books, magazines and flowers. As he seemed in no hurry to leave Northgate I suggested to him that his business might need his presence.

'Oh, I think they can get along without me for a while longer. I have a good manager. Besides, this is the first holiday I have had for years.'

★　★　★

The inevitable happened. We invited him to dinner. Our only other guests were two of our Northgate friends: Doctor and Mrs Purcell.

Mr Blackwood appeared to make a good impression.

'Rather charming!' pronounced Mrs Purcell in the drawing room afterwards. 'A forbidding exterior and an abrupt manner but something curiously attractive about him, don't you think?'

I was beginning to feel so myself. Sometimes I saw those dark, piercing eyes regarding me with an almost calculating expression and wondered what on earth he was thinking. I found out that very evening.

When the Purcells had departed Mr Blackwood lingered on until after eleven. Lucy was beginning to look tired and, hoping he would take the hint, I suggested she should go to bed.

'Yes,' he agreed, 'you mustn't stay up on my account, Miss Lucy. I am about to leave now — when I have had a word with your sister on a small matter of business.'

That startled me. What possible business matter could he possibly want to discuss with me late at night and why could Lucy not hear?

'What on earth can that be?' cried my sister. 'Are you going to offer Rachel a partnership in your gun business or is she to become an underwriter at Lloyds?'

'You will know in good time.' He smiled.

'I hope so, or I shall die of curiosity.'

When we were alone Mr Blackwood paced about the room without speaking and then came to the back of the sofa where I sat and leaned over me. When he laid a hand on my shoulder I felt a sensation so disturbing that I knew I ought to move away but I stayed where I was.

'Rachel,' he said, his head close to mine, 'I can't keep calling you Miss Garland, it makes you sound like a maiden aunt.'

'Which I will undoubtedly be eventually.'

'What makes you say that? You do yourself less than justice.'

'A plain woman over thirty has little else to hope for if she is honest with herself.'

'Over thirty you may be but plain you most certainly are not. I've never seen a woman with a finer figure and I'd call your face handsome enough for any man to admire. I may sound blunt but that's my way.'

I felt his fingers playing with my hair and then he kissed the side of my neck with some warmth. At last I found the resolution to break away, albeit somewhat reluctantly.

'Mr Blackwood, I really can't let you take liberties like this. If that was your intention when you asked for a few words alone with me then I think you had better take your leave at once.'

'I'm sorry, Rachel, if I have offended you.' His face was flushed and he moved round the sofa and sat beside me, seizing my hand so I could not escape.

'You haven't offended me,' I said, my voice unsteady, 'but I think I am entitled to an explanation of your conduct.'

'Can't you guess? Must I go down on bended knee?'

'If a gentleman makes advances to a plain, penniless spinster of thirty, then either he is short-sighted or — '

'What do you mean, penniless?' he broke in roughly.

'Well, not completely penniless as I have two hundred a year from Papa but — '

'Then how do you live in a house like this and keep servants and a carriage?'

'It's Lucy's money, not mine. We are half-sisters, remember. Our father was a country clergyman but his second wife was the only child of a Yorkshire mill owner who left Lucy everything he had.'

Even as I spoke my mind was racing. I had been expecting a declaration of love, a prospect that filled me with mingled excitement and alarm. Now, suddenly, he was glaring at me with scowling brows as though I had offered him some appalling insult.

'What's wrong?' I asked. 'What were you going to say?'

'It doesn't matter. I was under a misapprehension. I'm sorry if I upset you. I must go.' He departed abruptly with a hasty goodnight and not so much as a backward glance.

I went upstairs in turmoil and threw myself on the bed. For a long time I lay trying to calm myself. It was perfectly obvious that Nicholas Blackwood had been about to declare himself, perhaps even to propose marriage. It was equally obvious that he had changed his mind the moment I had revealed my lack of money. He was nothing more than a fortune-hunter!

How appalling if our relationship had developed further — perhaps even an engagement — and *then* he had found out the truth, as assuredly he would have done before long. I would have been jilted before all the world! As it was, no one need ever know. I had had a lucky escape. Of course, I would never see him again. I could not even tell Lucy, but I was sure Mr Blackwood would return home immediately so I would not have to trouble finding excuses.

I was hurt; not badly hurt perhaps, but I felt humiliated and rejected. For a few minutes I had thought an attractive man admired me, and, recalling the touch of his hand and his mouth pressed to my neck, I suppressed the shudder of delight that in all probability I would never feel again.

3

'What did Mr Blackwood want to speak to you about?' asked Lucy at breakfast the next morning.

'Oh, he changed his mind and left, so I am as much in the dark as you. He's a strange man, isn't he? Somehow I don't think we shall see him again.'

Lucy was aghast. 'Why ever not? You didn't quarrel with him, did you?'

'Of course not. Surely you won't be upset when he leaves Northgate? He's bound to go soon.'

'Yes, I suppose so.' Lucy's face was flushed and her eyes unusually bright.

'He's too old for you,' I said quietly. 'He must be nearly forty.'

She shrugged. 'I don't care about that. He's one of the few interesting people we know.'

I was not at that point much concerned with Lucy's feelings towards Nicholas Blackwood as I was sure our acquaintance was at an end. The next day, however, we encountered him in the town's circulating library. We were both engrossed in choosing our books and neither of us saw him until he suddenly appeared behind us and spoke.

'Good morning, ladies. Both well, I trust?'

For a few seconds I stared at him, astonished by his effrontery, and as I did not speak Lucy quickly engaged him in conversation. She was at her prettiest and most animated that morning, her head crowned with a straw hat trimmed with pink roses and ribbons, eyes sparkling and curls tossing. He smiled at her fondly and with a cold, sinking feeling, I began to wonder if he intended to transfer his attentions to my sister.

It soon became obvious that this was the case. Wherever we went he seemed to appear. I could not walk along the beach or down the high street without glancing apprehensively around, expecting to see that dark, broad-shouldered figure coming towards us or striding after us. I wrote a letter to him at his hotel asking him not to trouble us again, but it had no effect at all except to make him more persistent.

'Why don't we invite Mr Blackwood to dinner again?' asked Lucy, a few days after the encounter in the library.

'Because I do not want him to come here and I would feel a good deal happier if he kept away from us.'

'I thought there was something wrong. You

seem so cold towards him. Has it anything to do with that evening he was here and said he wanted to talk to you?'

'Yes,' I said. Reluctant as I was to reveal my humiliation I realized the time had come to confide in Lucy. If it would save her from developing an infatuation for this man, then it would be worth it. I told her all that had passed between us.

'It sounds to me,' said Lucy at last, 'as though you've let your imagination run away with you. I'm sure he can't have said all those things. You misunderstood. He didn't actually make you an offer of marriage, did he?'

'Well no, but — '

'There you are, then! I can't think why you should suppose him to be a fortune-hunter when he's a rich man.'

'So he has led us to believe. We've only his word for it. All that about his brother living in a castle — '

'It was built by their father. They made their money in arms manufacture. They must have amassed a fortune supplying guns to America in their Civil War. Mr Blackwood can afford to stay at the Belle Vue, at all events.'

'Seaside resorts can always produce a few men on the lookout for a wife.'

'And why not? There are plenty of people

on the lookout for a husband. I think he was probably trying to make himself agreeable to you in that rather brusque way he has and he was clumsy or tactless and gave the wrong impression!'

'Lucy, you have never before refused to take my advice; I am advising you not to see him again.'

'Why? Are you jealous?' Her cheeks were scarlet.

'How could you say such a thing?'

It was not like Lucy to be deliberately hurtful but I could see that she was in one of her stubborn moods. I suggested we might go away for a while: London, the Lake District, even France — anywhere she liked — but she declared she had no intention of leaving Northgate. I knew opposition might make her even more wilful so I said no more.

I did, however, send a note to the Belle Vue asking Mr Blackwood to meet me on the clifftop walk. Without Lucy knowing I slipped out of the house and went to the top of the road, where, beyond the last house, a path led through the rough grass and on the other side lay a vast expanse of sea. It was a windy day with dark clouds driven fast across the sky above the tumbling, white-edged waves below.

He came walking towards me with that

purposeful, vigorous stride, head thrust slightly forward. I suddenly thought of a bull about to charge. He seemed in high spirits for he grinned broadly as he took off his hat and his black hair ruffled in the wind.

'Good afternoon, Miss Garland! A wild day for wild words!'

'I don't understand.'

'Don't you? Surely you have called me here to give me a piece of your very well-ordered mind? No? Then perhaps I am to hope for a romantic assignation. Passionate embraces between sky and sea! I am at your bidding, dear Rachel.'

'I think you know very well why I wish to speak to you privately. After that unfortunate misunderstanding the last time we were alone together I fully expected you to leave Northgate. The fact that you didn't, and that you appear to be deliberately seeking us out, suggests that you have transferred your attentions to my sister. I have told her everything.'

'And considering the manner in which she has welcomed my company, it seems she hasn't taken much notice.'

'She is not used to dealing with men of your sort. I can only ask you, if you have any decent feelings, to leave her alone and go home.'

'So now I have been told,' he said with a sardonic smile, quite unembarrassed. 'The green-eyed monster, eh?'

'What! Do you suppose I am jealous of my own sister? All I want is for her to be happy. You flatter yourself that I care enough for you to experience jealousy on your account.'

'No, you flattered *yourself* that I was about to make an offer for your hand — you, the plain, over-thirty spinster as you described yourself. You had quite given up hope before I came along and although I may not be a handsome knight on a white charger I obviously aroused expectations.'

'How dare you! You are nothing but a common fortune-hunter prepared to marry anything in a skirt if she has significant funds.'

'Ah, now you are angry! You are much better-looking with colour in your cheeks and your hair loosened by the wind.'

We had been walking but now stood facing each other on the clifftop. I realized I could not argue with him: he had a sharp, sardonic answer to everything that was crude but effective.

'What you *really* want is this!' he said, and suddenly seized me in his arms and, despite my struggles, kissed me hard on the mouth; then he pushed me away and strode off

20

without another word.

I went back to the house wishing with all my heart that I had never asked to see him. For the second time he had succeeded in humiliating me. I had never encountered his like before; I was used to courteous, kindly men who considered my feelings and treated me with respect. And yet, beneath my helpless rage and misery there lurked a memory that would never quite leave me — the memory of the sensations awakened by that rough kiss on the windy cliff beneath the stormy sky.

4

My anxiety abated during the next few days. Much to my surprise Mr Blackwood had left town. I could scarcely believe that my words had had any effect on him but I thought he might have received a request to return home in order to deal with some problem in the family business.

Lucy could not accept that he had gone without a word but when several days went by without our seeing him or receiving any message, she insisted we call at the Belle Vue Hotel to make enquiries. We were told that Mr Blackwood had left the hotel four days previously and, as far as they knew, had returned home.

'How could he?' she cried, as we walked back to The Laurels. 'We had become such friends! And to go without a word — it's so rude!'

'He never struck me as a particularly courteous or considerate man,' I observed, secretly much relieved to be free of embarrassing encounters. I was also glad to see Lucy spared a possibly hurtful experience. She seemed angry rather than distraught but I wondered how much she was keeping to herself.

In the two weeks which followed she did not seem very well and had lost her appetite. She refused to see Dr Purcell and insisted there was nothing the matter with her, yet as her health was delicate I could not help but worry.

On Sunday Lucy pleaded a headache and missed church. She excused herself from a shopping expedition and an afternoon with the Sewing Circle and spent most of her time either in her room, lying on the sofa pretending to read, or wandering about the garden. I wondered how much she was missing our recent companion but she flared up at once when I mentioned his name and said she never wished to hear of him again.

When the day came for the Sale of Work at our parish church she declined to attend.

'I don't feel well enough. I can't stand about all afternoon.'

'We can find you a chair. You've been too much alone lately. The company and occupation will do you good.'

She shook her head. 'Give my apologies. At least I've made quite a few things for you to take.'

Mattie and I went in the carriage, loaded with boxes and baskets, the products of many hours sewing, knitting, tatting and embroidering. The afternoon passed slowly, as is usual on such occasions, and was surprisingly tiring. We were both glad when the carriage came to take us home.

When we arrived at The Laurels I asked the parlourmaid where my sister was.

'I've no idea, Miss Garland, I haven't seen her all afternoon. I expect she's in her room.'

I ran upstairs, partly from anxiety to discover if she was feeling any better, partly from eagerness to amuse her with an account of the afternoon's activities. Lucy's painted bookmarks and shell boxes had been a great success.

When I tapped on the door of her room and received no reply, I flung it open and stopped dead, at first bewildered and then frozen in horror. I turned and called for Mattie to join me and then stepped forward, surveying the chaos about me.

Clothes were flung on the bed, hatboxes emptied of their contents, gloves and handkerchiefs scattered on the floor. The room bore all the marks of a hasty packing and departure.

'What a mess!' was Mattie's first remark, but as she began to realize what the 'mess' signified her expression became grim.

'It looks as though Miss Lucy has left us,'

she said. 'I hope she's not run off with that Mr Blackwood. I don't care for him. I wouldn't trust him as far as I could throw him.'

As Mattie busied herself restoring some order to the room I went over to the dressing table, now denuded of its furnishings, and picked up the envelope I had seen propped against the glass. It was addressed to me and with a sinking heart I opened it, already able to guess its contents.

18th October 1867

Dearest Rachel,

This will come as a shock to you but please try to understand. I love Nicholas with all my heart and soul and I know you will not approve of our marriage so our only course of action is to marry and prove *ourselves happy. And I* am *happy, dear Rachel, happier than I have been in all my life before.*

Forgive me for the slight deceptions I have had to practise so that you would not try to prevent our union. I knew Nicholas had moved only a few miles down the coast and on those occasions when I made excuses not to join you, we met secretly — in the garden or in secluded places nearby.

We are to be married in London and then go to Paris for a honeymoon. After that we travel to Avalon Castle in Worcestershire. Imagine my living in a castle, even if it is quite a new one! Nicholas thinks it would not be good for my health to live with him in Birmingham. His house there is small with no garden and lacking in comfort. So I am to stay in the country and he will join me every weekend.

I will write again when we return from our honeymoon. The only thing I desire is to see you and embrace you and hear your words of forgiveness. I don't want to hurt or distress you but I believe you want me to be happy and so I am — deliriously, wildly, passionately happy!

Your loving sister,
Lucy

I sank into a chair, feeling as though my legs could no longer support me.

'Mattie, I am afraid your worst fears are realized. Lucy has run off with Mr Blackwood and they are going to be married. Here — you may read the letter.'

Lucy was of age, of course, and had inherited her grandfather's fortune of forty-five thousand pounds on her twenty-first birthday. I remembered my father being somewhat concerned about this, perhaps afraid of fortune-hunters, and suggesting it might be wise to make it twenty-five or even thirty. His father-in-law was adamant. He said that Lucy might well be married by then and be in need of money to set up home and provide for children. Somehow I don't think the old gentleman ever thought his beloved grandchild would run off with a highly ineligible suitor. There had been trustees, of course, who provided us with the funds to move to The Laurels and live in comfort but now Lucy had inherited it was too late to think of marriage settlements. Her fortune would be in the hands of Nicholas Black-wood.

Mattie handed the letter back to me with a frown. 'I hope she doesn't live to regret it,' she said.

'So do I!'

I realized my feelings towards Lucy had undergone a change. Although I still loved her as a sister I no longer trusted her. I felt let down. She had acted a part during the last couple of weeks and deliberately told lies to cover her deceit. I could forgive her but never forget her duplicity.

The next few weeks passed like an unpleasant dream from which I longed to wake. Nothing was the same yet the daily routine remained unchanged. I gained some relief from confiding in our friends, the Purcells, who were deeply shocked by Lucy's elopement.

'I didn't care much for the fellow, what little I saw of him,' confessed Dr Purcell, 'though I didn't say anything at the time because he was a friend of yours.'

'I must admit I thought him rather fascinating,' said Mrs Purcell. 'A complete rogue as it turns out, but who can tell? The whole thing may work out very well in the end.'

'It won't work out well for poor Rachel here,' said Dr Purcell, looking at me with something like pity. 'I'm sure you won't be able to live at The Laurels.'

This had already occurred to me. I had begun to visualize a future life in a small cottage somewhere with just Mattie for company. The Laurels was Lucy's house and so was everything in it, save for a few pieces of furniture which had belonged to my mother. It seemed all too likely that I would soon lose my home.

In mid-November a letter arrived at last from Avalon Castle, Kilwood, Worcestershire. Lucy assured me she was wonderfully happy and much impressed by her new surroundings. Nicholas's brother Ambrose was particularly warm and welcoming. She longed to see me and invited me to join her for Christmas, and to bring with me dear Mattie, whose attendance she greatly missed. I was to pack all her clothes and send them on to her as she had taken only a few essentials on her trip to London. Nicholas had bought her some wonderful new clothes in Paris but the old ones would do for every day.

At last came the expected and much-dreaded direction that the house was to be sold. She listed the items that she wished to keep — not many — and everything else was to go with the house.

It was at that point I broke down and wept. I was not only sorry for myself — that was the immediate and obvious cause for my tears — but I was possessed by an underlying dread of what was to come. I was convinced, despite Lucy's protestations, that nothing good could possibly result from this hasty marriage to a cold and mercenary blackguard.

5

Within a month the servants had been dismissed and the house sold. Dr and Mrs Purcell were very kind and undertook to store my few bits of furniture in their attic. I was not at all sure how long I would be staying at Avalon Castle and I had no wish to make arrangements that would be difficult to reverse. Perhaps a week or two in new surroundings would give me time to come to a decision about my future.

Mattie said little. She had always been a woman of few words but I knew she felt as apprehensive as I did.

'Miss Lucy has made her bed and she must lie in it!' she declared. 'God help her!'

We travelled by an early train to London where we obtained a connection to Worcester and then a branch line to Bromsley, the nearest town to Kilwood. We were met at the station by a handsome carriage sent by Ambrose Blackwood to convey us the two miles to Avalon Castle. The coachman wore a smart livery and I was favourably impressed. I had been inclined to think the wealth of the Blackwoods was a myth.

The December evening had darkened as we reached the end of our journey so we saw little of the surrounding countryside. We passed through two small villages, Monkstone and then Kilwood itself, but saw no people and few lights in windows.

'Wish we could see a bit more,' muttered Mattie. 'Not much life here by the look of it. I've had my doubts all along, I can't deny it.'

So had I, but Mattie was a born pessimist and I tried to sound reassuring.

'I'm sure everything will look better by daylight,' I said, with forced cheerfulness.

We turned off the main road and after driving some distance down a winding lane came to an imposing pair of gates which stood open for us. They were suspended on strangely turreted gateposts and flanked by Gothic lodges.

The drive was lined with great trees, now leafless, so that we were plunged into a dark tunnel from which we emerged into a circular carriage 'sweep' and drove up to a huge arched porch. The house was enormous, though we could see little of the outside in the gloom, which was relieved only by the glimmer of light from many windows.

'Miss Lucy was right, then,' said Mattie. 'It *is* a castle.'

'Well, yes, though it's quite a new one. It's

certainly much bigger than I expected.'

The door was opened and we were ushered inside by a stately butler and greeted by a smiling, pleasant-looking man who proved to be Nicholas Blackwood's elder brother.

There was little resemblance between them. Ambrose was smaller, slimmer and of lighter colouring. He was actually better-looking than his brother, with fine-drawn regular features. His expression was kindly and yet there was something lacking; the large hazel eyes were dreamy, the mouth sentimental. Nicholas had inherited all the energy and vitality and had they entered a room together there is no doubt who would be noticed first.

'I can't tell you how glad I am to have you here, Miss Garland!' he declared, seizing both my hands in his. 'Dear Lucy is still in the drawing room — ah no, here she is now to welcome you.'

Even as he spoke I could hear running footsteps and Lucy came rushing through an archway towards us, arms outstretched. Our greetings over, I looked at her anxiously, seeking some change, but her cheeks were flushed and her eyes sparkling.

'Oh, Rachel, do you truly forgive me? I was naughty, wasn't I? But everything's turned out for the best. You can see for yourself how lovely it is here — or you will tomorrow when we can show you the house and park in the daylight. It's like a place in a fairy tale.'

'More like a legend,' suggested Ambrose with a smile. 'I had in mind Malory rather than the Brothers Grimm.'

'Ambrose planned the whole thing himself,' said Lucy. 'I do think he's so clever — and he has more ideas for the future. Oh, I'm being so neglectful. This is Jessica, my *other* sister.'

She had been followed into the entrance hall by a dark, stout woman with a heavy-featured, rather sullen face. At first, noticing the bunch of keys which hung from a chain at her waist, I had assumed her to be the housekeeper. Her plain black dress with the lace collar pinned by a cameo brooch seemed to confirm this assumption and I found I was right.

Jessica Blackwood, the eldest of the family, had insisted on keeping house for her brothers. This somewhat eccentric arrangement seemed to work very well, I discovered, though there was an under-housekeeper to deal with some of the more mundane matters in the household.

Jessica's brusque manner of speaking and her dark, heavy-browed looks reminded me forcibly of her brother Nicholas.

'Come upstairs and have tea in my boudoir

— you must be longing for a cup after your journey,' said Lucy eagerly. 'And dear Mattie! It's lovely to have you with me again. Miss Blackwood will show you to your room. It's very nice and not too far from mine. Mattie's my old nurse,' she told Ambrose, 'and more of a friend than a servant. I don't know what Rachel and I would have done without her.'

I followed Lucy through the arches of the carved stone screen that filled the left side of the entrance hall and found myself in an astonishing lofty medieval hall with a hammer-beam roof and great windows full of heraldic glass. A huge fireplace built to accommodate half a forest blazed with a log fire and the walls were lined with tapestries, suits of armour and weapons of war that were all too perfect to be old.

Passing through a door at the end of the hall we emerged into a broad corridor with a great staircase leading upwards.

'Ambrose will show you over the house properly tomorrow. He'll enjoy telling you all about it. He had an architect draw up the plans of course, but all the ideas were his own.'

I was feeling stunned. I had convinced myself that Nicholas Blackwood's description of his family home had been a fantasy designed to impress, even though he had been rather sarcastic about his brother's artistic tastes, but this place was far grander than I could have imagined. I cannot say I greatly admired the style of architecture; it was too cold and gloomy and fanciful for my taste, but it was certainly impressive.

'The house was originally built by old Mr Blackwood, I believe,' I said.

'Oh yes, there was an old red-brick manor called Kilwood Hall but that was pulled down twenty-five years ago. The castle on the hill nearby was used as a quarry to provide the stone for the new house but the original was much smaller and simpler than this. Ambrose has completely transformed everything to suit his own ideas.'

'And do you like it?'

She hesitated only a second. 'Of course I do — it's so beautiful and exciting — like living in a poem or a novel. Nicholas thinks it's all a waste of money, but he's far more down to earth than Ambrose.'

We reached the top of the stairs, where corridors led round a great central courtyard. I looked through one of the windows and saw a cloister garth with a lawn, a fountain and a statue of a knight holding a sword.

'King Arthur,' explained Lucy. 'Ambrose is quite besotted with him. I'll show you to your room first and then we'll have tea.'

My room was on the south side of the house with a beautiful oriel window looking out over the park.

'Very splendid!' I observed, noting the peacock-blue draperies and Gothic carving. 'It will be like sleeping in a cathedral.'

'Rachel!' said Lucy, in a quite different tone of voice. 'I'm so sorry if I hurt you, truly I am. I know how anxious and upset you must have been. And I've made you sell our house and brought you to live in a strange place. Now you can see how happy I am, can you forgive me?'

'Of course I forgive you. How could I do anything else?'

We embraced and the little awkwardness that had attended our reunion vanished. Yet at the back of my mind a certain doubt persisted. Lucy certainly looked happy and well but a bride of two months would scarcely have had time to find out whether she had made an appalling mistake. My mind would not be set at rest until I had seen her living with Nicholas Blackwood. So far, it seemed, he had treated her kindly. I asked no more.

'I'm so glad to have Mattie back!' Lucy declared. 'Now I can get rid of that smart French maid we took on in Paris. Poor Berthe has been so unhappy here. She does nothing but cry and the fact she speaks very little

English makes it worse. I'll give her a glowing testimonial and send her home.'

We took tea together in Lucy's boudoir at the rear of the house.

'I never had a boudoir before,' she giggled. 'It makes me feel like the Empress Josephine. I suppose it's really just a sitting room but I'm to have it fitted out to my taste when my new furniture arrives. I want a great deal of blue, don't you think? A pretty blue! I don't much care for this sage green Ambrose seems to like so much. He calls this room my bower, would you believe. But that's so like him. Did you notice all the rooms are named after people in the legends of King Arthur? I'm in Guinevere.'

'Then you are obviously meant to be the queen of the castle!'

'But Nicholas would make a poor King Arthur. He'd say Excalibur was useless and produce the latest make of rifle. Anyway, I suppose Ambrose is the king.'

'He seems very pleasant.'

'Oh, he's a darling! Though he does have a bee in his bonnet about the house. It's a sort of dream castle where he can pretend to be a Knight of the Round Table or something of that sort. All quite harmless.'

'But expensive.'

'I suppose so, but the Blackwoods are very

rich. They made a fortune out of the Crimean War and another out of the American one.'

'Now that's over I suppose there will be less demand for guns.'

Lucy shrugged. 'There's always fighting going on in some part of the world.'

'Ambrose doesn't actually have anything to do with the business?'

'No, he's not at all interested. Old Mr Blackwood left the estate and a half-share in the business to Ambrose and the other half-share to Nicholas.'

'Lucy,' I said, hesitatingly, 'a little while ago you mentioned bringing me to live in a strange place. I understood I was being asked to stay as a guest over Christmas — nothing more.'

'But surely you'll stay longer than that? I hoped you'd stay here more or less permanently. I need company when Nicholas is in town all week.'

'Surely that depends on Ambrose — and your husband too, of course.'

'They won't mind, I'm sure.'

I was not so certain and although I was anxious to keep an eye on Lucy, I was not too taken with the idea of being a permanent companion living in a mausoleum of a house. However, I decided such matters could wait and we finished our tea and cake in almost the pleasant amity of past times.

Afterwards, when I returned to my room, I found that my luggage had been unpacked and there was nothing left for me to do but wash and change for dinner.

The meal was served in a palatial room panelled in dark oak with a vaulted ceiling and a sideboard like a church organ. The food was excellent and Ambrose Blackwood a charming host. His sister Jessica sat at the table with us but said very little and didn't smile at all.

Afterwards we three women sat in the drawing room, a vast shadowy apartment where no one could ever be comfortable. Ambrose did not wait long before joining us and I was glad to see him. I could not talk easily to my sister in front of Jessica, who was so grimly taciturn that even occupying the same room seemed like hard work. I got the impression she did not approve of Lucy and me but perhaps she did not approve of anybody.

While she was dispensing tea and coffee, a woman entered the room and addressed herself to Ambrose, speaking so quietly that only he could hear. She was about thirty years old and of striking appearance: small, slender and sallow of complexion, with black hair drawn back tightly from her face. She was not at all pretty but there was something sensual in the heavy-lidded eyes, the slightly arched nose and full red lips. There was a hint of the foreign about her — Spanish or Italian perhaps. Her dress was plain but well made and not that of a servant. Over it she wore a striking and expensive paisley shawl in shades of red and purple.

'What did she want?' demanded Jessica Blackwood when the woman had departed as quietly as she came.

'Alice isn't very well so Miss Carr has sent her to bed. Some trifling thing — no more than a headache, but she wouldn't eat her supper.'

'She should have been *made* to eat it,' declared Jessica. 'That child is too much indulged.'

'Oh come,' smiled Ambrose, 'I'm sure I don't want to eat if I feel indisposed.'

'That's different. You dose yourself with that nasty laudanum. She's only eight years old and shouldn't be allowed to have her own way. And that Miss Carr takes too much on herself. She gives herself airs and is far too opinionated for a governess. I'll have to have another word with her.'

'My dear Jessica,' her brother protested mildly, 'she is a well-educated and intelligent woman. As such she is perfectly entitled to have opinions and I really do not think we have grounds to criticize her work.'

Jessica sniffed. 'That's as may be, but I've always said she was a wrong'un and I don't care who knows it.' She darted a glance towards Lucy and me on the sofa.

I had at least been relieved of the necessity of asking who the intruder might be. Alice was, I recalled, Nicholas Blackwood's daughter by his first wife. I wondered briefly why Lucy had not mentioned her; after all, the child was her stepdaughter. I was about to say something and then changed my mind. It was, I sensed, one of those subjects best reserved for when Lucy and I were alone.

That night, before going to bed, I stood for a while at the window of my room. The moon was almost at full and all was at peace, yet I felt anything but calm. From first setting foot in the house I had experienced a sinking unease and this was not entirely to do with the oppressive style of architecture. I had a disagreeable, rather sinister fancy that I was waiting for something to happen. I had no idea what, save that it was likely to be deeply unpleasant.

6

Next morning I woke feeling far more cheerful and went down to breakfast with a good appetite. Afterwards Ambrose offered to show me over his castle and talked with such enthusiasm I was inspired to express approval although I still disliked the style of the house.

Later, as the day was fine, he suggested a walk in the park. He conducted me by the lake, and showed me the boathouse where two handsome vessels were housed: *Golden Wings* and *The Blessed Damozel*.

'We use them more in the summer,' he explained, 'though we took one out on a fine afternoon to give your sister a taste of pleasures yet to come. The lake freezes in cold weather and if the ice is safe we can skate.'

'I've never skated. I'd like to try,' I smiled.

'I can teach you. It's great fun, though I'm afraid Jessica doesn't approve.'

'That must be only one of many things.'

He chuckled. 'I can see you've got her measure already. She's not the merriest of souls, I must admit, but she has a good heart under that gruff manner and she is my sister, after all.'

We entered a small copse where trees and bushes grew thickly. There were many evergreens and even on a bright morning such as this a gloomy, dim light prevailed.

'This is the grotto.' Ambrose indicated an artfully constructed rocky pile. 'It was built before my time and I believe it was intended as a summerhouse, but it's in the wrong place. My father said there was some sort of room at the back but it's so overgrown you can't see anything of it. We have a much prettier summerhouse by the lake. Let me show you.'

He really was a charming man and I wondered why he had never married. Possibly Lucy could tell me. Perhaps he was awaiting the advent of some Guinevere or Iseult who was unlikely to appear outside the pages of a medieval romance.

On our return to the house I went upstairs to take off my bonnet and cape. As I crossed the landing I heard someone singing in a strange, plaintive little voice. I changed direction and turned down the corridor where the schoolroom and nursery lay. Ambrose had, of course, confined his tour to the main part of the house but he had shown me the plan of each floor.

I stopped, listening; the voice was much clearer now and seemed to be coming through one of the doors. Softly, I turned the knob and peeped in. A pale-faced little girl with straight dark hair was standing in front of a piano, picking out a tune as she sang.

'Lady Alice, Lady Louise,
Between the wash of the tumbling seas
We are ready to sing, if so ye please
So lay your long hands on the keys — '

She was quite oblivious to my presence and I stole closer. This was obviously the schoolroom but there was no sign of Miss Carr the governess. It seemed a strange occupation for an eight-year-old girl to choose.

'And ever the great bell overhead
Boom'd in the wind a knell for the dead,
Though no one toll'd it, a knell for the
    dead.'

'That's a very sad song for one so young,' I said gently.

She started a little but did not return my smile. A plain child, I thought, despite those large dark eyes.

'Uncle Ambrose composed the tune and

taught me to play it.'

'Did he write the words too?'

'No, they are by Mr Morris, a friend of my uncle's. He's an artist and a poet.'

'You must be Alice. I am Rachel Garland, your father's sister-in-law.'

'Yes, I saw you arrive yesterday but you didn't see me. You don't look at all like my stepmother. She's very pretty.'

'She is, isn't she? That's because we are only half-sisters. That is, we had the same father, but not the same mother.'

'So if she and my father had a little girl, it would be my half-sister?'

'Why yes, of course,' I said, rather disconcerted by this turn in the conversation. 'I hope you are feeling better now,' I added. 'We were sorry you could not join us in the drawing room yesterday.'

'Not really. No one cares about where I am or what I'm doing — not even Papa.'

I was shocked. 'I'm sure that's not true, Alice; he must love you a great deal.'

She shrugged. 'I don't know about that. He didn't care much for Mamma. Nurse says he made her cry. I had a little sister, you know. Her name was Louise — Lady Alice and Lady Louise, like the song. But she died when she was only three days old and Mamma died soon afterwards so I'm half an orphan.'

'That's very sad. You must miss your mother.'

'I do, but she was ill quite a lot. I always remember her in bed or propped up with pillows in a big chair, doing embroidery.'

'Have you any recollections of her that are less melancholy?'

She shook her head. 'Not really.'

'But that was two years ago. You must try to be more cheerful. Couldn't you find something more light-hearted to sing?'

'I don't know anything.'

'Come now, I'm sure you do.' I played a few bars of 'The Grand Old Duke of York'.

'That's a nursery rhyme!' she said with scorn. 'I can read Shakespeare. And I can play the piano quite well for my age, or so I'm told. I wasn't really trying just now.'

At that moment the door flew open and Miss Carr sailed in. She stopped abruptly when she saw me.

'I've just been having a little chat with Alice,' I explained. 'I heard her singing and thought it was time we were acquainted.'

'Singing? She was supposed to be writing.'

'I've finished that,' said Alice.

'I'll soon find you something else to do,' promised Miss Carr.

'I'd better go,' I said, making for the door. 'I hope we may talk again soon, Alice,' I added, and nodding at Miss Carr I departed.

Later, as we walked in the park, I told Lucy of the episode. 'She seems an odd little girl.'

'Very odd,' agreed Lucy. 'I can't get anywhere with her. I did so hope we'd be friends. I mean, I didn't expect her to call me Mamma or fall into my arms the first time we met but she's very difficult. She just stares at me with those great eyes and either says nothing at all or makes disconcerting remarks.'

'Perhaps it's the result of being alone so much with that governess and never mixing with other children. I don't think I like Miss Carr, which is unfair because I've scarcely spoken to her.'

'Your instinct is right. I detest the woman!' Lucy spoke with some heat.

'Has she done anything to annoy you?'

'Nothing specific but I always feel she's mocking me. She looks so vindictive and hostile sometimes — I can't think why. Perhaps it's just her expression but I don't trust her.'

'Has she some foreign connection? She doesn't look English.'

'I believe her father was some sort of wine merchant whose business failed. Her mother was Spanish so I suppose that accounts for her appearance.'

'Could you arrange for Alice to meet other children?'

'There aren't any. The vicar and his wife are elderly and our nearest neighbour, Mr Norton, is a bachelor.'

'Perhaps a good school — '

'I ventured to suggest that idea but Nicholas wouldn't hear of it. He says Miss Carr is very clever and accomplished and can teach her better than any schoolmistress. He may well be right. I'm sure she's very competent and one can't insist on someone's dismissal simply because one doesn't like the look of her. I don't see much of her anyway.'

'I don't think Jessica thinks much of Miss Carr. You may have an ally there.'

'I'm not sure Jessica approves of me. She cares for nothing but running the house. Apparently there used to be a proper housekeeper but Jessica criticized and interfered so much that she resigned and Jessica took over. She's not a person to cross. Anyway, it's really nothing to do with me, is it? At least Ambrose is always kind and considerate.'

'I'm surprised some enterprising lady hasn't snapped him up. He'd make a very good husband.'

'He would, wouldn't he? But Nicholas told me that he was disappointed in love. He wanted to marry Mr Norton's sister Helena from Monkstone but she went off to Italy and married an Italian count. She's supposed to be very beautiful and alluring.'

'Oh, poor Ambrose! Let's hope he gets over it and eventually finds someone suitable to be chatelaine of his dream castle.'

'She might not want to live in the same house as two sisters-in-law and a difficult child. But then it's not at all likely at present. I'd rather not think about it. Nicholas seems convinced Ambrose is doomed to remain a bachelor — ' She broke off suddenly. 'What was that?'

'Nothing — only a rook. You seem to have a lot of them here. What's the matter? You've gone pale.'

'It startled me — rocketing out of that bush and making that horrible noise.' She glanced round anxiously and looked up at the windows of the house as though searching for something.

'What is troubling you?' I asked. 'Lucy, my dear, I am the one person in the world you can trust absolutely, you know that. Are you truly happy?'

'Of course I'm happy,' she snapped. 'And nothing is troubling me. Why do you ask?'

'You seem a little nervous. I wondered if anything was causing you anxiety.'

'I just wish Nicholas was here, that's all. I do so miss him.'

I was unconvinced. Lucy seemed quite out of place in this strange world she had entered. Apart from Ambrose, who spent half his time lost in fantasy, there seemed no one who wished her well. She was surrounded by a vague atmosphere of hostility. Perhaps matters would improve when her husband returned but I doubted it.

7

That night, when the whole house was in darkness and all its inhabitants fast asleep, I was wakened abruptly by shrill screams coming from another room.

I jumped out of bed, snatched up a shawl, and ran to the door. I heard footsteps and voices calling and then saw the glimmer of a candle coming round the corner of the corridor. It was Jessica, whose room was at right angles to mine.

'What is it?' I cried. 'Who was that screaming?'

'It came from over the other side. I hardly think it was Ambrose so it must have been your sister.'

I rushed to Lucy's room, overtaking Ambrose on the way. She was standing in the doorway in her nightgown, whimpering. When I spoke to her she threw herself into my arms and burst into tears. For a while I could get no sense out of her, and Jessica helped me to take her back into her room while Ambrose went to fetch Mattie. Soon the candles were lit and I could see nothing that was at all alarming or out of place.

'A nightmare!' I told Lucy. 'It's a long time since you had one of those.'

Privately I thought that sleeping in such a room was enough to give anyone nightmares. The bed stood on a dais, draped with crimson and purple damask. The ceiling was fan-vaulted with carved heraldic bosses and the fireplace seemed to have wandered in from a cathedral tomb. The furniture was painted with dim little pictures of Arthurian knights and damsels, all of a rather sickly aspect, and one wall carried a painting showing the death of Guinevere.

I thought of Lucy's room at The Laurels in Northgate, so fresh and pretty with its rose-sprigged wallpaper and muslin curtains. I wished with all my heart that she was safely back in it.

Mattie arrived with smelling salts and sal volatile and Ambrose fetched brandy, but even without these restoratives Lucy seemed calmer. Presently she apologized for disturbing us and asked to be left alone.

'Not you, Rachel!' She caught me by the hand. 'Please stay with me a little longer.'

When the others had gone she said in a low, tremulous voice: 'I don't know if it was a nightmare or not but I was so frightened. It's not the first time I've seen her — there were two other occasions.'

'Seen who?'

'I beg you not to make light of it, Rachel. Sometimes I wonder if I'm going mad, having hallucinations . . .'

'I can't help you if you won't tell me.'

'But I *want* to tell you! I can't keep it to myself any longer. Did you know this house was supposed to be haunted? And don't say it's nonsense.'

'I won't! Although it is a little unusual for a new house to be haunted, you must admit. Who or what is the ghost?'

'Nicholas's first wife.'

'And who told you this?'

'Alice.'

'You believe a fanciful child?'

'She only told me what all the servants believe.'

'What form does this haunting take?'

'Esther Blackwood is seen in her wedding dress and veil. She was buried in them, apparently. Usually she appears at night but occasionally during the day.'

'You say you've seen her three times. Tell me about it.'

'The first time I saw her gliding along the corridor as I was going to bed one night. The second time I was outside the house in much the same place where we were this afternoon when the rook startled me. I saw her at the window of this room — over there in the oriel. Then tonight I woke up and found her standing by the fireplace.'

'You were alone each time?'

'Yes. Do you think I imagined it?'

'No. Did you see her face?'

'Not properly. The first time she had her back to me. The second time I was too far away. Tonight she had a lace veil over her face and the moonlight shone on her through the window. I'd drawn the curtain back to let in a little light — it's so very dark in here.'

'Has anyone else ever seen her?'

'One of the maids and the housekeeper who resigned. I know she didn't get on with Jessica but that wasn't the only reason she left.'

'Is there a picture of her anywhere?'

'Alice has a small portrait of her in her room and there's a photograph of her in the dressing room.'

I fetched it at once, and sitting on the edge of Lucy's bed I held it out so that we could examine it together. Esther Blackwood had been no beauty. I could see where Alice had got her thin, pinched little face. She looked at least forty.

'She was older than Nicholas.'

'About four or five years, I think. She was forty-two when she died.'

'She looks meek enough. What sort of person was she?'

'I don't really know. Nicholas never mentions her and I suppose Ambrose and Jessica would think it tactless. I get the impression she was a quiet, inoffensive sort of woman.'

'Then not one to be afraid of in either life or death.'

'You don't think I'm going mad, do you?'

'Of course not. Don't talk nonsense.'

'But you don't believe in ghosts!'

'I believe people see ghosts but that's not the same thing. There could be several explanations. Perhaps someone wishes to frighten you.'

'I hadn't thought of that.'

'The figure you saw wasn't transparent?'

'No, quite solid. At least . . . the veil gave a rather misty outline.'

'And it didn't suddenly vanish?'

'No, it simply glided out of the door. But why should anyone — '

'That's something we'll have to find out. I'm sure it was a real person. Now, try to get back to sleep. I'll stay with you, don't worry.'

'I feel much better now. I shall lock the door in future.'

'Yes, my dear, that's a good idea.'

I sat beside her until she fell asleep and

spent the rest of the night on the couch in the dressing room with the door open.

The next morning Lucy was bright and cheerful and inclined to laugh at the night's horrors.

'I really made a fool of myself, didn't I? Ambrose and Jessica will think me a very silly sort of wife for their brother. If he'd been here I'm sure it wouldn't have happened.'

She was, I thought, a little *too* bright to be entirely convincing, though the sun streaming through the windows was enough to make the events of the previous night seem like a bad dream. I was less sure. If someone *was* trying to frighten my sister I was determined to find the culprit.

8

When we were in the drawing room the previous evening Lucy and I had planned to take a walk to Monkstone if the weather was fine. As it was only a week until Christmas it was time to think of decorating the house. Holly, ivy and other evergreens could be brought in from the park by the gardeners but we had no mistletoe. Jessica told us that there were old apple trees at Monkstone which always carried 'that parasite'.

'I'm not sure it's the right thing to have in a Christian house,' she declared. 'I'm sure it's pagan. Something to do with Druids.'

'It probably is,' said Lucy, 'and my papa would never allow it in his church, but a bunch inside the front door and another in the hall would be suitably festive and no harm to anyone.'

'May I come with you?' Alice cried out suddenly from her seat in the corner with Miss Carr.

'Certainly not!' her governess intervened. 'You have your lessons tomorrow morning. Come along now, it's time you were in bed.'

The next day, however, Lucy breakfasted in

bed and declared herself too weary to walk to Monkstone. The events of the previous night had upset her more than she was willing to admit and despite her pretence of cheerfulness she looked pale and drawn.

'You go, Rachel. It's a pretty walk and you can ask about the mistletoe. We could send someone over to collect it.'

She announced her intention of spending the morning in her boudoir with Mattie and perhaps taking a gentle stroll in the garden in the afternoon. I decided to do as Lucy suggested as it was a bright sunny day and the walk to Monkstone and back would fill the time very pleasantly until luncheon.

I took a path through the park to a side gate in the form of a stile, below which wooden steps bridged the ditch into the lane. As I wished to reach Monkstone by another route than the main road, Lucy had advised me on the best way to take.

Only when I was away from Avalon did I realize how oppressive I found the place; sunlight and birdsong are great revivers of low spirits. I felt free and slightly reckless as I walked briskly to the end of the lane; there I found another path which branched off through an apple orchard, where I saw many bunches of mistletoe growing from the older trees.

There was no one in sight so I continued my walk until I reached Monkstone, which proved to be a pretty village built around the River Rode. I made my way to the church, which was a small Norman building, quite plain inside with one massive archway and whitewashed walls. There were a few memorial tablets to members of the Norton family but nothing more elaborate. I looked at my watch and decided it was time to go home. I thought I would follow the path through the wood as Lucy had said how picturesque it was.

When I left the church I saw an ancient manor house half-hidden among the trees. It was long, low and timbered, its leaded windows twinkling in the sun. This had to be Monkstone Hall, home of William Norton, bachelor.

The walk through the woods was delightful and I came at last to a rustic bridge across the water. Lucy had told me it was one of her favourite spots and I was to look out for a kingfisher. I crossed halfway and stood gazing at the curve of the sun-dappled stream. Something vividly blue streaked along the surface. I leaned forward eagerly and the rail on which my arms were resting suddenly gave way and I plunged forward into the water.

I cried out with the shock of it, wallowing about like a porpoise, except that porpoises are not encumbered with clothes. I could not have drowned, the water was too shallow for that, but I had some difficulty clambering out and I was in a disastrous state, shaking with shock and cold. My hat had gone, my hair had escaped its pins and was dangling wetly about my face and my soaked skirts were so heavy they weighed me down. I struggled to the bank, seizing tufts of grass and weeds to drag myself up, where I found a large, hairy black face close to my own and a wet pink tongue obligingly trying to dry my nose.

'Nero!' a voice bellowed and the dog backed away. My arms were seized in a firm grip and I was hauled to safety. My rescuer was a tall, heavily built man about forty years old with a cheerful, weather-beaten face that was some distance from handsome. He wore a shabby tweed shooting jacket, breeches and gaiters.

'What a pickle!' he exclaimed, in a deep voice that seemed on the verge of laughter. 'This is not the place to go swimming, my dear lady. Here — have a sip of brandy.' He produced a pocket flask.

'The rail of the bridge gave way when I leaned on it,' I explained, after choking on a mouthful of spirit. I began to wring out my skirts as well as I could.

'Really? That's strange. I leaned on it myself only yesterday; it was all right then and my weight is considerably greater than yours. I'm very sorry it should happen as this is my property and I do try to keep everything in good repair. However, the least I can do is take you to my house and see you are given dry clothes and taken home.' He took off his jacket and placed it round my shoulders.

'Can you walk? You aren't hurt apart from the soaking? Good! Just as well it's a mild day. Come along.'

It really was an extraordinary situation, I thought, as I stumbled along at his side, my skirts flapping heavily against my legs. I did not dare to think what I looked like, yet here I was, soaking wet, walking through a wood clinging to the arm of a man I had never seen before in my life.

'My name is Norton, by the way. I live at Monkstone and the house is quite near. You are a stranger here, I believe?'

'Yes, I've just been visiting your village. I wanted to get some mistletoe but I couldn't find anyone to ask so I was on my way back to Avalon Castle. I'm staying there with my sister, Mrs Nicholas Blackwood. I am Rachel Garland.'

'Oh yes, of course, I might have known. We are to meet more formally tonight as I am coming to dinner. Well, who would have thought it? We'll certainly remember our first meeting. A really original introduction, if a trifle damp. Just as well I heard you cry out, though it was Nero who reached you first, so he must have the credit. He's a very good swimmer, being a Newfoundland. They have webbed feet, you know. He would soon have rescued you.'

We arrived at the timbered manor house I had seen earlier and I was handed over to the care of Mrs Morgan the housekeeper, who took me up to a bedroom, provided me with hot water and towels and then brought me some of her own clothes while mine were being dried in the kitchen.

My hair was the greatest problem but I dried it as well as I could and, as I had lost most of my pins, tied it back with a ribbon provided by Mrs Morgan. She told me that Mr Norton would like to see me downstairs in the morning room, which proved to be a small, panelled chamber with windows overlooking the garden. The furniture was a curious mixture of every period with curtains and covers of old faded chintz, but the general effect was very pleasant.

'My dear Miss Garland, I think you had

better have a drink to guard you against catching cold.'

'Thank you, but not brandy again, please.'

'Then Madeira perhaps.'

The heavy sweet wine was warming and cheering. I began to feel a great deal better.

'Do you wish to go home immediately, or shall I send a message explaining where you are and then take you back to Avalon this afternoon?'

I hesitated. I had taken an instant liking to Mr Norton and his house but I felt I ought to return to Lucy.

'As you wish,' he said, 'but you see the fire is lit and I think you should sit by it for a while to make sure you are quite warm and rested. Your hair is still damp and it may not be advisable to go out again until it is dry.'

Eventually I found myself agreeing to stay for luncheon at Monkstone, and a message was sent to Avalon Castle saying I would not return until the afternoon and asking for some of my own clothes to be sent.

'This is very agreeable and quite a change for me,' said Mr Norton, as we sat on either side of the Pembroke table that had been laid for us by the fireplace.

'You live alone, I believe?' I said. 'Have you no family?'

'I have a sister but she lives in Italy.'

'Really?' I recalled Lucy telling me something of the sort. 'That's rather unusual.'

'We have an aunt who has lived in Florence for years for the sake of her health. She invited Helena to stay with her. There was an ulterior motive from the first, I suspect. At all events, within a year Helena became the Contessa d'Ortoli.'

'How grand!'

'Well contessas are not as rare in Italy as they are in England. The Count was considerably older than my sister but a decent man by all accounts. He died last spring and Helena is thinking of returning to Monkstone, at least for a while. The estates went to a cousin but she inherited a house in Venice and a generous annuity. I am going to fetch her home in the New Year if the weather stays clear.'

'Has she any children?'

'No; if there'd been a son he would have inherited and I suppose Helena would have felt obliged to stay in Italy. As it is, she's young enough to start a new life here. I'd rather hoped she'd marry Ambrose. He was always devoted to her and despite his eccentricities he would have made her a good husband. One never knows — perhaps his chance will come again.'

After the meal he took me over the house.

It was very old; parts of it dated from the fifteenth century but most had been built in the time of Queen Elizabeth. Everything in it seemed well worn and rather shabby. There was comfort but no ostentation.

The drawing room was long and low with a large bay window at one end with modern sash windows reaching nearly to the floor. Mr Norton explained that these improvements were made for the benefit of his mother, who was a keen watercolourist and did exquisite embroidery.

Before throwing open the door of the library my host shaded his eyes with his hand in mock shame.

'This is my lair. I do hope you are not excessively tidy by nature or you'll think me lost beyond redemption.'

I peeped in and saw a book-lined room piled high with yet more books on the floor, on chairs and on tables. Papers and documents were scattered on the large mahogany desk and on the carpet all round it.

'No one's allowed to put things in order or I'd never find anything. A little light dusting once a week is all I permit.'

I laughed; there was something very droll about his manner and it was obvious he did not really care what anyone thought of him. It suddenly occurred to me: this is a gentleman's house as Avalon Castle can never be.

Afterwards Mr Norton drove me home in his gig. I was now wearing my own clothes which had been sent from the castle. We were carrying a large load of mistletoe. I found myself remarkably at ease with him, as though I had known him for years. He was fond of reading and his taste was so far-ranging we had much to discuss. As he dropped me off at the porch I felt the anxieties that had been troubling me return as though a grey cloud had settled over my head.

'I won't come in now. We'll meet again this evening. Goodbye, Miss Garland.'

I found Lucy in her boudoir, still looking rather pale and listless, but she seemed amused by my adventure.

'He *is* nice, isn't he? I think William Norton would do very well for you, Rachel. Why didn't I think of it before? It would be lovely if you could live at Monkstone.'

'Don't be silly, Lucy!' I said, more sharply than I intended.

'You've gone quite red. Now that's unusual; you hardly ever blush.'

I suppose I ought to have felt pleased that Lucy was so much recovered from her fright that she was able to laugh and tease me but I found myself irritated and annoyed. If I probed a little deeper and tried to discover why that was I would realize it was because she had put my own thoughts — not yet admitted — into words.

There was something about William Norton that I had found instantly and irresistibly attractive. His very presence was cheerful and comforting, unlike the disturbing sensations aroused by Nicholas Blackwood. I told myself it was unlikely I could ever be more than a friend to Mr Norton but I would settle for friendship.

9

That evening we had three guests to dinner: the local vicar and his wife and William Norton. The Reverend Arthur Hobbs was elderly, quiet and dull and obviously dominated by his wife, who talked for both of them. Mr Norton looked slightly uncomfortable in evening dress but he smiled cheerily when he saw me.

'None the worse, I see. Indeed, a tremendous improvement!' He came over to me, hand outstretched.

'Thank you,' I replied, 'I feel a great deal more like my usual self now.'

'One thing I noticed after you'd gone,' he murmured, steering me into one of the window embrasures. 'I went back to the bridge and hauled out the fallen rail. It looked to me as though someone had deliberately loosened it. Those light pieces of wood are only nailed into place but they are usually quite firm if they are not treated roughly. There were fresh marks of a chisel or something of the sort where the nails had been prised loose.'

'But why? Mischievous boys, do you think?'

He shook his head. 'Boys, if they dared to do such a thing, would want to see the result and enjoy a laugh. I swear nobody was about when I found you. Besides, if that bridge is crossed more than once a day it would be busy. Who would want to wait for hours on the chance of someone falling over?'

'I don't understand. What are you trying to say?'

'Only one or two people are likely to have used that bridge today: myself and a gamekeeper perhaps. Not many people go to Kilwood that way: the main road is so much quicker.'

'You mean someone deliberately wished to hurt a particular person?'

'I don't know any more than you but I am considering possibilities. It's feasible one of my gamekeepers is the subject of some rural revenge or that I have some unknown enemy with a grievance. Otherwise that leaves you and your sister. You told me that originally you both intended to walk to Monkstone and that the bridge was one of your sister's favourite spots.'

'Yes, but I am a stranger. Who would want to harm me? And as for anyone wanting to injure Lucy — the idea is laughable.'

'Is it?' he looked serious. 'Hasn't she told you?'

'Told me what?'

At that point we were interrupted. Ambrose was showing Mr and Mrs Hobbs some new treasure he had purchased and called us over to express an opinion. I was troubled by what Mr Norton had begun to tell me and glanced at the high-backed settle where Lucy sat, her face pale but smiling.

There was no opportunity to talk privately with Mr Norton after that as dinner was announced but I thought I might contrive a word with him later in the drawing room. Halfway through the meal I thought I heard the sound of a carriage outside and before long a message was brought in that Mr Nicholas Blackwood had arrived from Birmingham and would be joining us shortly.

I knew, of course, that he came home every weekend and was to stay longer over Christmas but no one had mentioned his absence and as time passed I thought that perhaps he was not coming after all. Indeed, I hoped this might be so as I was dreading my first meeting with him. However, it had to be faced sometime and if I could avoid speaking to him alone, which I supposed would be easy enough, I would feel a good deal more comfortable.

He entered ten minutes later, apologized gruffly for not being dressed for dinner, dropped a perfunctory kiss on Lucy's brow and sat down in the empty chair next to me, much to my dismay.

Soup was brought, although we were now on the pudding, but he waved it away and asked for meat and vegetables. He addressed himself to the food without speaking to anyone and I was certainly not going to force him into a conversation if he preferred silence. I continued to chat in a desultory fashion with Mr Hobbs on my left.

'It's been a day of minor disasters,' said Lucy brightly. 'First my nightmare, then Rachel falling into the stream and then Alice slipped on the back stairs and bumped her head. And Jessica broke a cup — though that was rather an anticlimax of course . . . '

Nicholas Blackwood set down his knife and fork and stared at her. 'What are you talking about? What nightmare? What bumped head? What falling into streams?'

Lucy explained. There was something strange about the manner of it, I thought. She was overeager to amuse him and to make light of her own weakness. I had no doubt she was afraid of someone else — the surly Jessica perhaps — telling him of the night-time disturbance. As for his scowling reception of her story, it seemed positively angry.

The man's a barbarian, I thought. He

might at least show a little sympathy.

Later in the drawing room, Miss Carr brought in Alice for a little while and everyone looked at the bruise on her forehead, which had been liberally anointed with arnica. She seemed to enjoy the attention, maintaining the air of an invalid, which made Mrs Hobbs compare her to her poor mother. I managed to speak to her away from the others for a few minutes and learnt a few facts that seemed significant.

Miss Carr sat in the window embrasure with some crochet and took no part in the conversation, but when the gentlemen came in she rose and carted Alice off to bed, despite the child's pleas for a longer stay with the grown-ups.

It was some time before I contrived a few words with Mr Norton and I at once asked him what he had meant earlier when he questioned my belief that no one would want to harm Lucy.

'I thought she might have mentioned it to you,' he said. 'It happened a couple of weeks ago and she was badly frightened at the time. She was locked in the boathouse by some mischief-maker and it was never discovered who was responsible. Her cries for help were not heard and it wasn't until dinnertime and quite dark that anyone realized she was missing and a search was begun. Fortunately, it was a mild day so no harm was done but it must have been a very disagreeable experience.'

'What on earth was she doing there in the first place?'

'Oh, there'd been a boating picnic in the afternoon as the day was so sunny and warm for the season and Ambrose was anxious for her to experience the pleasure of floating on the lake before the boats were put away for the winter. She suddenly remembered she'd left her shawl in *Golden Wings* and went back to recover it. I can't think why she didn't send a servant but I wasn't here and I'm only repeating what Ambrose told me.'

'I seem to remember him telling me the names of the boats.'

'Something to do with poetry.'

'So I believe. But it's strange that Lucy hasn't mentioned the episode. Still, I haven't been here long and we've had so much to talk about. She obviously doesn't think the subject very important.'

'Perhaps. I almost wish I wasn't going to Italy in the near future. You may have need of a friend in the neighbourhood. However, judging from this morning's incident you do not appear to be unduly nervous or easily alarmed.'

'I'm not sure I understand you.'

'It's all right. I think I've said too much already. But I must say I rather enjoyed our adventure, though it was unpleasant for you in many ways. It's not often I can play the knight errant and despite Ambrose's efforts to found a new Camelot there's not much opportunity for rescuing damsels in distress in this part of Worcestershire.'

'What do you know of Miss Carr?' I asked abruptly, anxious to return to the possible source of the trouble.

'What does anyone know of Miss Carr? She's been employed as Alice's governess for more than two years and as far as I know she has discharged her duties conscientiously. She's an intelligent woman, though not one I would care to cross. I've always fancied she's something of a spitfire. Perhaps I'm unjust.'

'No, I have the same impression. Have you any idea how she was given the post? Did she answer an advertisement?'

'I think not. She was employed by the Weston family at Bishop's Green, which is about five miles from here. Their daughters were nearly grown up and they no longer needed a governess. I think Nicholas got to hear of it and arranged for her to come here. Until then Alice was taught by her mother. Why the interest?'

'My sister doesn't like her and I must admit it crossed my mind that Miss Carr might be responsible for the accidents that have befallen us. I had a word with Alice before you joined us. Miss Carr was late for breakfast this morning; they usually have it in the nursery. The poor child went looking for her. That's when she slipped on the back stairs and Miss Carr, who is usually very punctual, came charging up the steps, all breathless and dishevelled, and picked her up. She'd obviously been out of doors.'

'You think she could have gone out early and damaged the bridge?'

'It's possible. Lucy and I discussed walking that way yesterday evening. But I would hate to throw suspicion on someone who is innocent so I'd better say no more about her.'

Mrs Hobbs came bustling over at this point to tell us that Ambrose was going to sing for us and asked if I could play the piano.

'Only adequately, I'm afraid.'

'I'm sure you play very well, my dear. Mr Blackwood has a beautiful voice and I am venturing to sing myself, though my talents are rather more limited.'

She was right, but Ambrose had a very sweet tenor and concluded their recital with a couple of songs of his own composition, including the melancholy air I heard Alice playing the first time I saw her. Nicholas Blackwood deliberately, and quite ostentatiously, left the room before the performance started.

When our guests departed Nicholas appeared again, bade them a perfunctory goodbye and declared his intention of having a smoke before retiring. It seemed that Lucy would be alone for a while so I went to her room and found her in her dressing gown, brushing her hair. Mattie had been putting away her evening dress and wished me goodnight before departing.

'You look very tired,' I told Lucy, 'and you scarcely ate a thing at dinner.'

'I'm perfectly all right, especially now Nicholas has come home. He's staying now until after Christmas. Isn't that wonderful?'

'I'm surprised he can leave the factory for so long.'

'Oh, but it isn't a factory. Gun manufacturing is carried out in lots of individual workshops. He has to visit them all, of course, and attend to all the accounting and office work, but he has a very good manager so that there's no need for him to be there all the time.'

'Lucy, I've been talking to Mr Norton and he told me that you had a rather unpleasant experience which involved being locked in the boathouse.'

The hairbrush stopped for a moment on its downward path and then continued, more slowly.

'Oh, that! It was of no consequence. Someone must have thought the place was empty and locked up.'

'Do you know who?'

She shrugged. 'I can't see that it matters. One of the servants probably, too embarrassed to own up. I couldn't have come to any harm. It was a mild day for the time of year. I had my shawl and there were cushions and a rug in the boat. It was just extremely boring, that's all.'

'Mr Norton seems to think it was more serious than that.'

I wondered if I ought to mention the loosened rail of the bridge but then decided I had better not. I knew Lucy so well that I could tell when she was putting a brave face on. She was *too* dismissive and nonchalant and I had no wish to alarm her, especially after last night's terrors.

'Mr Norton is a very nice man but it's really none of his business,' she said, laying down the brush.

'Well, at least you won't be afraid tonight, with your husband to protect you.'

'Oh yes, any self-respecting ghost would run away screaming at the sight of him.'

'Even the ghost of his first wife?'

She reddened. 'You seem to think it was someone playing a trick — unless you secretly believe I dreamed the whole thing.'

'No, I never said that. I'll go now, Lucy, I don't want Nicholas to find me here.'

'Why not?'

'I don't want him to think I am going to interfere or influence you in any way. I'd rather he didn't find us having private talks too often or he might misunderstand. I do not imagine him to be excessively tolerant.'

'He is very good to me, Rachel. I love him and I'm sure that when you know him better you'll grow to love him too. It's just his manner that sometimes gives people the wrong impression. Please don't say anything to him about what happened last night. I've told him I had a nightmare and woke up screaming. We'll leave it at that.' She paused, then added, 'He never mentions his first wife. I tried to ask him about her once but he refused to say anything and grew quite angry. I think he was badly hurt.'

I nodded and said goodnight without further comment but as I was closing the door behind me, I saw Mattie stealing down the passage, beckoning me to follow her.

'There's something funny going on,' she whispered. 'Come and listen!'

Mattie's room was in the nursery wing which ran along one side of the courtyard on the first floor. It was just beyond the schoolroom where I had first encountered Alice. Between this and Mattie's door lay another room to which she pointed meaningfully.

There was no need for gestures; I could hear only too clearly the sound of two angry voices — that of a man and a woman. I followed Mattie into her room and quietly asked why she had fetched me.

'It's *her* room — that Miss Carr's. And he's in there with her — Mr Blackwood!'

'Mr Ambrose Blackwood?'

'Of course not. I mean Lucy's husband.' Mattie picked up a tumbler, placed it against the wall and applied her ear.

'Mattie, you shouldn't!'

'Shhh!' Her face was screwed up in concentration like a wrinkled apple.

It was undoubtedly Nicholas Blackwood's voice, I could tell that now: it was too rough and deep for Ambrose. Miss Carr sounded shrill and demanding, though I could not tell a word either was saying. I could only suppose he was angry with the governess over some aspect of her work or her treatment of his daughter and she was vigorously defending herself. It was rather odd that he should choose to visit her room in order to speak to her: an interview in the schoolroom or the library would be more appropriate. And why at this time of night when everyone was going to bed? Miss Carr had retired some time ago and by now could well be in her nightdress. I began to wonder . . .

Miss Carr certainly did not sound like a dutiful governess. Judging by her tone of voice and the vehemence of her replies she was giving as good as she got. There was a sudden crash as though something had been hurled across the room; then the door opened and closed with a resounding slam. Silence followed and Mattie removed the glass with a puzzled expression.

'I can't make it out. I couldn't hear very well, the wall's too thick. But I heard a few words. They were having an almighty row.'

'That was obvious.'

'She'd done something he didn't like.'

'That too was obvious. He was probably angry about Alice falling on the stairs. Perhaps he thought Miss Carr wasn't looking after her properly.'

'I didn't hear him say anything about that. The words I heard were 'She's my wife!' and Miss Carr said, 'Do you think I haven't noticed?' Then a little later he shouted, 'If you don't behave yourself you can go — I'll even give you a reference.' She said, 'Go? You'd never dare dismiss me.' That was about all but it proves what I suspected. There's something funny going on.'

'Yes,' I said. Privately, I had come to the same conclusion some time ago; this was merely another piece of the puzzle.

'Shouldn't be surprised,' added Mattie in a whisper, 'if there's some sort of dalliance between that hussy and Mr Blackwood. No governess would be so familiar with her employer unless he'd been more than that.'

Similar thoughts had occurred to me but I simply bade Mattie goodnight and went to my room. No one was in sight in the dim corridors. Nicholas Blackwood must have joined Lucy for the night. I could not suppress the thought that she was afraid of him. My poor sister! I felt sure there were difficult times ahead for her and problems which even those who loved her would not be able to solve.

10

The next morning, as it was Sunday, Lucy and I walked with Ambrose to the village church, followed by Miss Carr with Alice. The latter carried a small posy of Christmas roses and ivy, which puzzled me until after the service. Nicholas declined to accompany us and Jessica had taken herself off to the Methodist chapel at Bromsley, accompanied by Mattie. The two of them seemed to have struck up an odd sort of friendship.

Kilwood Church was old, but curiously unattractive. There was something wrong with the proportions and the various alterations made over the centuries had been carried out with a clumsy hand. However, I thought that a few hundred pounds well spent could improve the building and I wondered that Ambrose, with his supposed love of the Middle Ages, did not spend a little on his parish church.

Yet was it so strange? I was beginning to realize that the ancient past he worshipped had no connection with reality. The peeling plaster, leaking roof and rattling windows meant nothing to him. His mind was full of fantasies of some beautiful, mystical world that had never existed, save in the pages of Malory or Tennyson or the strange, dreamy pictures of the artists he patronized.

Afterwards Alice wished to visit her mother's grave, so as Miss Carr was anxious to return home I offered to accompany the child. The old Kilwood Hall had belonged to an ancient family, now extinct. There were several monuments to them in the church and in the graveyard stood a large mausoleum where the last members of the line had been laid to rest. Near the churchyard wall were more recent graves and here we found the one we were seeking.

In Loving Memory
of Esther Blackwood
died 7th June 1865.
Also of her daughter Louise
aged three days.

There was no mention of husband or surviving daughter, no text or verse, and the headstone was extremely plain. Long grass had grown around it, whitened by the overnight frost. Alice took away some dead flowers and replaced them with her posy.

'Does your papa ever bring flowers?' I enquired.

'Oh no, he says it doesn't do any good but Aunt Jessica says I ought to do it and I *want* to.'

'That's the best reason of all.'

'Miss Carr doesn't like coming here. She says graveyards make her feel ill. I'm glad I don't have to walk back with her. She's in such a bad temper lately I can't do anything right.'

Lucy seemed in rather low spirits and sat about listlessly for the rest of the day, making no attempt to read or sew and scarcely joining in the conversation.

'Are you all right?' I asked her at one point.

'Of course!' she snapped. 'Is there any reason why I shouldn't be?'

That evening, however, as I prepared for bed, Lucy came to my room looking as she used to do when she was a little girl and sorry for some misdemeanour.

'Oh, Rachel,' she sobbed, 'I'm so wretched. Jessica said the most dreadful thing to me after luncheon.'

When I finally learnt what the 'dreadful thing' was it seemed no more than a crass remark from a blunt and outspoken woman with no tact: a suggestion that my sister seemed to be a useless young person.

'She's rather odd,' I said, 'but I'm sure she means no real harm. Perhaps she was upset by some trouble with the servants and wanted to vent her anger on someone. Don't take it to heart, for heaven's sake.'

'But there's worse,' she gulped. 'She suggested Nicholas only married me for my money.'

I was sure this was true but I could hardly say as much. I had warned Lucy of Nicholas Blackwood's mercenary ambitions before she so foolishly ran off with him. It was too late now to say, 'I told you so!' For some time I talked to her quietly and I think I was beginning to convince her that the insults were unintentional when we were interrupted by the door being flung violently open.

'There you are!' cried Nicholas Blackwood, bursting into the room like a charging bull.

'Mr Blackwood!' I was so angry I could scarcely speak. 'Do you normally rush into a lady's room without knocking? I'm not used to such extraordinary conduct.'

He ignored me at first, taking hold of Lucy by the wrist and drawing her after him. 'Come along, you should be with me, not that interfering sister of yours.'

'How dare you!' I exclaimed.

'How dare *you*! Remember what I told you. I will not have you two prattling and tattling behind my back!'

He left the room as swiftly as he had

entered it, Lucy casting on me a look so bewildered and alarmed that it was all I could do not to run after her.

Afterwards I realized that his rudeness was intentional: he wanted to be rid of me. I had no wish for similar scenes in the future and I found myself shaking and close to tears. There was nowhere I could go for comfort and advice. My only friend in the neighbourhood would be leaving shortly and there was no one in the house, save Mattie, in whom I could confide.

The future seemed bleak. I had a little money, enough to rent a cottage somewhere or take lodgings back in Northgate, but I was reluctant to leave Lucy. I would stay a little longer, I decided, even if I had to endure her husband's insults. I comforted myself with the thought that Nicholas was not in permanent residence at Avalon Castle and his brother's kindness was some compensation.

I lay awake most of the night and only fell into an uneasy doze at five, from which I awoke unrefreshed and low in spirits. Lucy breakfasted in her room but when I went downstairs I found to my relief that Nicholas had gone out early.

Ambrose was alone at the breakfast table, smiling and agreeable as usual. Noticing that I ate little he enquired after my health.

'I'm quite well, but not very happy at the moment,' I said. 'Unfortunately, your brother and I do not seem to have 'hit it off', as the saying goes. Last night he burst into my room without knocking when Lucy and I were talking, and almost accused me of interfering in their marriage and trying to influence her. It isn't true. I want nothing but her happiness and I feel he knows that very well.'

'Do not trouble yourself too much about Nicholas. He has a very blunt and aggressive manner at times. That's why he's the businessman of the family, I suppose. For that matter, he's often like that with me but I've learnt to ignore it. I know, for example, that he will be strongly opposed to my building a chapel here and will have some harsh words to say on the subject of my sanity, but that's his way.'

After breakfast I went up to see Lucy, who was reclining languidly on a chaise longue in her boudoir, looking pale and heavy-eyed but with a curiously self-satisfied expression.

'Are you well?' I asked her. 'After that outburst last night I feared the worst.'

'I can't imagine what you mean. I'm perfectly well, just rather tired. I didn't sleep much.' She smothered a yawn.

'Lucy, if he's unkind to you, I must know.'

'Unkind? No, he's not like that. You don't

think he beats me, do you?' She giggled a little. 'Quite the reverse but you couldn't possibly understand. And as for saying you *must* know, that's the very thing he warned me against. He said you'd try to turn me against him.'

'How could you believe that? All I meant was that I'm concerned for your happiness after so hasty a marriage.'

'I *am* happy — incredibly happy. Perhaps that's the trouble. There's bound to be a certain amount of envy, isn't there, when the younger sister marries first.'

I could scarcely believe it was Lucy speaking; then I realized it wasn't. She was repeating what he had told her. Lucy had always been somewhat pliant and easily influenced and it was clear she was besotted with him.

I said, quietly, 'One day you will find out how wrong you were. I hope the discovery will cause you no regret.' Then I left the room, feeling quite desolate.

It was not until dinner that evening that I saw Nicholas Blackwood again. Tea was served afterwards in the drawing room, and I wandered over to one of the great oriel windows where books and journals lay on an oak table. As I was turning over the pages of the *Illustrated London News*, a voice said, close to my ear: 'I hope you've recovered from the shock you suffered last night when I entered your room.'

'Of course.'

'Then to what must I attribute the baleful glances darted in my direction so many times? If looks could kill ... Are you practising to turn me to stone?'

'I don't know what you mean.'

'Of course you do, Miss Garland!' His hand clamped over mine. Angrily I tried to release myself, looking round for assistance, but the others were gathered round the piano at the other end of the room.

'Let me go, you're hurting me!'

'Not yet. It's the first chance I've had to speak to you alone. I know what you think of me and I just want to warn you.' His voice was low, almost guttural.

'Warn me? Of what?'

'Warn you not to interfere. Lucy is happy enough and I'll see that she remains so as far as I can, but I don't want you prying and meddling.'

'I wouldn't dream of such a thing. But your way of showing her care and consideration was very impressive last night.'

He chuckled. 'How little you know! I assure you Lucy passed a very agreeable night after I removed her from your room. I've never pretended to be Sir Galahad at King Ambrose's Round Table.'

'No, I'd never supposed your strength was as the strength of ten because your heart was pure.'

'Ah, I like that quality in you! But do as I say and all will be well, and remember that you are no longer responsible for Lucy. She is entirely mine!'

He turned abruptly and strode off, leaving me seething with anger and indignation. I hated him and I had never hated anyone in all my life before.

11

Christmas proved to be a dismal affair. Indeed, it was almost disastrous. Had Ambrose been content to follow more modern traditions all might have been well but he was determined to hold a lavish entertainment after the fashion of the Middle Ages.

A Christmas tree had been put up in the drawing room for the sake of Alice, and family gifts placed beneath it. Jessica dismissed it as a sinister foreign custom and she didn't care if it had been introduced by Prince Albert; it was still a nasty German idea and probably pagan. This was, however, the only concession to the sort of Christmas we usually celebrated.

Ambrose had the great hall decorated with greenery and issued invitations to all his respectable neighbours within a ten-mile radius. Few accepted. Some declined owing to age or illness; others pleaded previous engagements, having already arranged festivities with their families. Eventually only ten guests arrived, including the Reverend and Mrs Hobbs and Mr Norton.

Although a blazing fire had been kept going for days the hall was still rather chilly except in the immediate vicinity of the fireplace. The village band arrived with the church choristers and performed carols. This went off well enough, though I thought they shouted rather than sang and suspected a preliminary visit to the alehouse.

Then everything began to go wrong. Ambrose had appointed Joe Hicks, a jolly-looking stable boy, as the Lord of Misrule. He was drawn into the hall astride a monstrous Yule log, dressed in a particoloured costume with a jester's hat on his head and waving a pig's bladder on a stick. The band played 'God Rest Ye Merry Gentlemen' and the log was heaved onto the fire, which immediately began to go out.

A large wassail bowl was brought in and another vessel full of steaming punch. A game of snapdragon was announced, which was greeted with cries of horror from the ladies. The gentlemen did their best to seize the raisins through the flaming alcohol but did not appear to be enjoying themselves.

In the meantime the Lord of Misrule was running round the hall belabouring the guests with his pig's bladder. There were resounding shouts of 'Get away from my wife, you rogue!' and shrieks from their unhappy spouses, who beat off the fool with their fans.

Ambrose looked increasingly desperate. His brother glared at him beneath lowered brows; Jessica sat with her arms folded, determined to be miserable. Alice laughed, but more at the discomfort of the grown-ups than the antics of the prancing boy. The ladies began to send for shawls and capes until Mrs Hobbs loudly asked Ambrose if they might move to a warmer room.

'It really is a very cold night and some of your guests are well advanced in years. This may well have been the thing in ancient times but modern people have some idea of comfort.'

Ambrose confessed himself defeated and I felt quite sorry for him. The band, the choristers and the Lord of Misrule were paid off with ale and half a crown each for their efforts and we all traipsed into the drawing room to play forfeits and charades. No one wanted blind man's buff so we sat around trying to amuse each other with guessing games.

Later we repaired to the dining room for supper and our company revived considerably under the influence of champagne. When the meal was finished those who had been obliged to travel made their excuses and with appropriate thanks wished everyone a merry

Christmas and departed.

William Norton lingered behind to talk to me.

'I'm sorry I must be going,' he said, 'but I have much to do. I leave for Italy in two days.'

'So soon?'

'Yes, I shall spend the winter there and return with Helena in the spring, so I'm afraid we shan't see each other until then.'

'I envy you,' I said. 'I would love to travel.'

'Perhaps you will one day. Goodbye, Miss Garland, and a happy Christmas.' He took my hand in his and held it for a little longer than necessary. Then he glanced up and steered me beneath the large bunch of mistletoe that was suspended in the porch.

'I must take advantage of the season,' he said, 'especially as I have provided the where withal.' Then he bent and kissed me. I was expecting a peck on the cheek and was surprised but not at all offended when his mouth encountered mine very gently, but at some length.

'I enjoyed that,' he smiled. 'I hope to do that again one day — without the mistletoe. God bless you.'

With those words he took his leave. I was sorry to see him go: he seemed to bring with him a welcome air of good humour, sanity and common sense, all of which seemed in short supply at Avalon Castle. There was now something else too but I did not dare to hope.

It was now after eleven and there was little point in prolonging the festivities, such as they were, although Ambrose wanted us to sit up until midnight telling ghost stories.

'No!' cried Lucy. 'I'm going to bed. I've had enough of this nonsense and I'm very tired.' She took Nicholas's arm.

Alice had been packed off earlier and there was no sign of Miss Carr.

'That's the best idea I've heard yet!' declared Jessica, making for the stairs.

'That leaves only us,' I said sadly to Ambrose, who was looking very downcast.

'The whole idea was a mistake. Modern people simply can't enter into the spirit of our ancestors.'

'Nothing could have been like your imagination,' I said, 'so perhaps it's better to leave it there.'

'You're probably right. I suppose you want to go to bed too?'

'Would you mind?'

'Of course not. I'm afraid this evening's disappointments have brought on one of my headaches. I usually sit for a while in the library with the window open until I hear the Christmas bells across the fields, but this year

I think I'll take a dose of laudanum and go straight to bed.'

'Then I'll open my bedroom window and listen for you,' I told him.

He smiled and wished me a happy Christmas. Then he bestowed a light, brotherly kiss on my cheek.

Two kisses in one evening, I thought, as I made my way upstairs. Yet that of William Norton, although equally gentle, had produced an entirely different effect.

Christmas Day itself passed in a more conventional manner. We attended church in the morning; even Nicholas joined the party. Later there was a lavish dinner with turkey, goose and a plum pudding. There were exploding crackers which Jessica refused to pull and a liberal supply of alcohol which she did not imbibe, but which had a cheerful effect on the rest of the company. We all trooped into the drawing room in a much-improved frame of mind.

The presents beneath the tree were then distributed by Ambrose. I had paid a hasty visit to Bromsley, the market town some two miles distant. I was not expecting much choice but I had brought a couple of items with me from Northgate and I was pleased to find a bookshop where I purchased *Alice in Wonderland* for Alice and a box of stationery for Ambrose. I resented having to buy anything for Nicholas but for Lucy's sake I thought I should. The same shop sold paperknives and one of them, with a nicely carved handle, seemed quite adequate.

At another shop I acquired an umbrella to accompany the monetary present I always gave Mattie, and I thought the satin handkerchief sachet I had made for the Northgate bazaar but never finished would do nicely for Jessica now I had embroidered her initials on it. That left Lucy. I had purchased from the best shop in Northgate a glove box inlaid with mother-of-pearl. Inside lay a pair of white kid gloves.

The distribution began. Miss Carr was looking particularly striking with her dark hair more loosely and elegantly arranged than usual and a large crimson bow at the neck of her grey silk dress. On closer inspection I saw that she was wearing earrings. She usually wore very small gold ones but these were larger and set with amethysts and pearls. I wondered how she had acquired them. There was little of the governess in her appearance, an impression noted by Jessica, who muttered under her breath, 'The hussy is getting bolder. I'd send her packing if it was left to me.'

She had not given me anything, which did

not surprise me, but thanked me grudgingly for the sachet.

'You made it yourself, I can see. Very nice! I like to see a young woman who can sew and make herself useful.'

This observation did not extend to Miss Carr, who had distributed modest handmade gifts to everyone.

I received a book from Ambrose, nothing from Nicholas, a pincushion from Alice and a beautiful fan from Lucy, who had brought it back with her from Paris.

The final parcel proved to be Nicholas's present to my sister. She tore off the paper and a flat oval leather box was revealed. On opening it I watched her face as I could not see its contents. A fleeting expression of disappointment was quickly replaced by a delighted false smile.

'Oh, Nicholas, how lovely — a parure! I've never owned anything so splendid.'

The parure proved to be a set of garnets: necklace, earrings, brooch and two bracelets. Lucy hated garnets; she always considered them to be 'old women's jewels' and indeed they were unsuitable for one of her age and colouring.

'They belonged to his first wife,' said Jessica in a loud whisper. 'Waste not, want not.'

'Let me put them on for you,' said Nicholas, busying himself with removing her pearls and replacing them with the second-hand garnets.

But then, I thought maliciously, he's second-hand too!

After Boxing Day Nicholas returned to Birmingham. Lucy maintained that she was delighted with his present but I noticed that she never wore any part of the set when he was not there. A pretty writing box from Ambrose pleased her more.

The weather changed in the second week of January. It had been cold over the Christmas season with flurries of snow and Ambrose hoped the ice on the lake would be thick enough for skating. Then it became milder, almost springlike, which drew grim predictions from Jessica.

'March in Janiveer, January in March, I fear.'

'I was hoping to learn how to skate,' I observed to Lucy, 'but I suppose the winter's not over yet.'

'I don't care. I wouldn't be able to take part anyway,' she replied.

'Why not?'

She shrugged, but I thought she had not been looking so well lately. I soon found out the reason. For several days she did not come down to breakfast and Ambrose asked if she was ill. I went up to her bedroom and found her, still in her dressing gown, sitting in a high-backed chair with a towel across her lap and a bowl on the floor beside her. Mattie was in attendance with smelling salts and sal volatile.

'How are you?' I asked anxiously.

'It's nothing. I've been like this for a while on and off.'

'The sort of illness young married women commonly suffer from,' said Mattie.

'Do you mean you are — '

'Going to have a baby,' said Lucy, smiling faintly. 'In about six months, I think.'

'Does Nicholas know?'

'I think he suspects but I haven't told him yet. I haven't told anyone except Mattie, who guessed straight away. You'll keep quiet until I say so, won't you, Rachel?'

'Of course, if that's what you want.'

'He'll be pleased; he'd like a son.'

'It could be a girl.'

'Then he'll make a great fuss of her.'

Would he? I wondered. He paid scant attention to the daughter he already had, apart from buying her an expensive present from time to time.

Despite Lucy's injunction to keep her secret for the time being, there soon grew a rumour in the household concerning Mrs Blackwood's interesting condition. There were sly looks, smirks and innuendos. Lucy seemed oblivious to all this until Jessica asked her bluntly if she was 'in the family way'.

The next weekend Lucy told her husband of her expectations. He seemed delighted and treated her with great tenderness and patience. I began to think that this hasty marriage might turn out well after all. However, it was after his return to town that disaster struck.

One night in the first week of February we were all awakened by frantic cries for help. Everyone who heard them ran out to discover what had happened. We found Lucy lying at the foot of the stairs in her nightgown. Between hysterical sobs she stammered that someone had pushed her downstairs.

12

It was some time before we could get any sense out of Lucy. At first we thought she had broken her leg but it proved to be a badly sprained ankle. She was obviously severely bruised and whimpered as she was carried upstairs by one of the footmen.

Worse was to follow. She suffered a miscarriage and the family doctor was urgently summoned from Bromsley. Mattie had already dealt with the worst consequences, assisted by one of the more mature female servants.

Dr Sawyer was elderly, kindly and rather old-fashioned, and he gave Lucy a sedative, bandaged her ankle and gave instructions that she was to rest in bed and be kept very quiet. He promised to return the following afternoon.

'I was pushed,' muttered Lucy as she began sinking into unconsciousness. 'That woman in the veil — she pushed me downstairs.'

'You go to sleep, my dear. No harm can come now. We'll stay with you.'

'Mattie,' I said, when my sister was asleep, 'what *did* happen?'

'We'll have to ask her when she's able to tell us; I don't know any more than you.'

'The last time she woke us in the middle of the night she swore she'd seen a ghost. She thought it was the spirit of her husband's first wife as she was in a wedding dress and veil and she couldn't see the face properly. I told her I was sure someone was playing a trick on her.'

'It's that Miss Carr, I'll be bound. She's a nasty piece of work and I wouldn't put anything past her. She's jealous of Miss Lucy. I've told you before what I think of her and Mr Nicholas Blackwood.'

I thought it quite likely, especially when I remembered the new amethyst earrings and the second-hand garnets.

Early in the morning a servant was despatched to the post office in Bromsley to send a telegram to Nicholas's Birmingham office, asking him to return to Avalon Castle immediately.

In the meantime poor Lucy was propped up on pillows and coaxed to eat a little scrambled egg for her breakfast. She only managed a few spoonfuls and a cup of tea and then gave way to weeping. Her face was very pale with dark circles under her eyes.

'She's lost a lot of blood, poor lamb!' said

Mattie. 'She needs beef tea.'

'Lucy,' I said quietly, holding one of her hands between mine, 'we must know what happened.'

She swallowed hard and then made a great effort.

'I couldn't get to sleep, I don't know why, but I lay for a long time counting sheep, dozing and then waking. Then I heard a strange noise in the passage out there — a sort of sighing, moaning sound. I thought at first it might be Alice — you know what an odd little thing she is — so I went to the door and opened it. Then I saw this veiled figure glide to the top of the stairs.'

'Weren't you frightened?'

'Not as much as last time because, after what you said, I was sure it was someone dressed up and trying to frighten me. Besides, I wasn't trapped in my room, I was out in the corridor with other people close at hand and I could shout for help if necessary. Anyway, it was moving away from me so I found enough courage to follow at a distance. When I reached the top of the stairs it seemed to have vanished. I was still hesitating on the top step when I was pushed.'

'You are quite sure of that?'

'Of course I am! You do believe me, don't you, Rachel? I am lying helpless here and there is someone in this house who tried to kill me!'

I did my best to reassure her but it was difficult to know what to say. Attempts to question her further resulted in wild sobbing so I said we'd discuss the matter further when she was stronger. Presently she fell into a light sleep and I beckoned to Mattie. We withdrew to the adjoining dressing room.

'What do you make of it?' I asked her.

'Well, she *was* pushed, I believe that. Whoever did it could have stood at the side of one of the suits of armour at the top of the stairs and then stepped out behind her. It was no ghost, of that I'm sure, but I've found out one thing about his first wife.' She nodded towards the chest of drawers where the silver-framed photograph of Esther Black-wood stood.

'She was an heiress,' Mattie continued, 'but after he married her it turned out that some of her investments were worthless and a bank failed. I don't understand such matters but she wasn't rich after all. Then he insured her life for a lot of money and then she died.'

'In childbirth, Mattie, and she was over forty,' I said, unwilling to entertain such suspicions as her words implied.

'It wasn't quite like that.' Mattie's face looked even grimmer. 'She had a bad time with the baby and it died when it was only a few days old. It was a small, sickly thing and it had to be baptized in a hurry.'

'Louise,' I added, 'a girl called Louise.'

'How did you know?'

'Alice told me and it's on the gravestone. Is there more?'

She nodded. 'The poor woman seemed to be getting over it and then she had a relapse. Sickness and pain and such-like and a fever. She was in such a weak state she couldn't stand it and died. I suppose it was natural but it was very convenient for *him*.'

'Mattie, you mustn't think such things.'

She shook her head. 'I don't trust anyone in this house. I'm going to keep a close eye on Miss Lucy from now on.'

'Until her husband arrives. We both know what he's like. He won't want either of us hovering around.'

She sniffed. 'He's not here all the time, thank heavens, and in any case he doesn't frighten me. Even his own sister doesn't trust him.'

'Miss Blackwood? Did she tell you all this about the first wife?'

'Of course, I don't listen to servants' gossip — they usually get things wrong. I know most people don't like Miss Blackwood but she's a good woman. She has principles and she tells the truth. She wouldn't accuse her brother of anything but she doesn't have a good word to say of him. There's bad blood in the family, that's how she put it.'

Nicholas returned in the late afternoon, shortly after Dr Sawyer had paid his promised visit, and charged up the stairs two at a time. He burst into Lucy's room like a tornado and I could hear him raging through the open door.

'My poor, poor little darling! What you've suffered! Don't cry, sweetheart; someone played a wicked trick on you. I'll find out who did it, never fear. Someone shall pay for it — for you and our poor child!'

His reaction was that of a devoted husband concerned only for the safety and happiness of his wife. Yet I wondered, suppose Lucy had been killed? I had no doubt he would display all the signs of grief but I did not doubt he would have suffered more sorrow had her money vanished.

What followed was even stranger than Lucy's experience. Miss Carr disappeared.

13

I first learned of the latest development when I returned to my room after breakfast and found Alice wandering along the passage.

'Have you seen Miss Carr?' she asked. 'She didn't join me for breakfast in the nursery and I wondered if she was ill so I was going to see if she was in her room. When I saw you coming up here I thought I'd ask you first.'

'Let's see, shall we?' I said, leading the way to Miss Carr's room, which was next to Mattie's.

'I love *Alice in Wonderland*,' said Alice. 'It's the best book I've ever read. Miss Carr flicked through it and said it was nonsense but if you chose it I don't think it can be.'

'I bought it for you to enjoy,' I said, 'so it's served its purpose.' I tapped on the door and called Miss Carr by name. Alice did the same. There was no reply.

'Perhaps she *is* ill,' I said, and cautiously opened the door. There was no one there. Not only that, but the room showed evidence of a hasty departure. The bedclothes were in a heap, the wardrobe doors stood open and there were odds and ends scattered over the floor: a book, a stocking, a glove, a scrap of tissue . . .

'All her clothes have gone!' exclaimed Alice. 'And her big trunk and most of her books — no, there's a pile of them here in the corner. I wonder why she didn't take them.' She poked her head into the wardrobe and brought out a pale bundle.

'This is all that's left. I don't know what it is but it can't be important or she'd have taken it with her.'

The parcel was tied carelessly together with a piece of tape. When I investigated further I found it contained a white flounced petticoat, a camisole and a large lace tablecloth. This, I felt sure, was the ghostly costume assumed by Miss Carr when she frightened my sister. I had no doubt now that it was she who had pushed Lucy downstairs.

'Do you suppose she's gone away forever?' asked Alice.

'I shouldn't be surprised. I rather think your papa dismissed her.'

'Her trunk's gone at all events. She always kept it in here; she said she needed it to store things in and she could keep it locked. Aunt Jessica said it was a poor, cheap thing, only wickerwork covered with brown canvas, but it was quite big. If that's gone I suppose she's not coming back.'

'Are you sorry?'

'Not at all. I didn't like her very much. She must have gone very early this morning, without saying goodbye to me or leaving a letter. At least, there isn't one here or in the schoolroom.'

'If she was dismissed very suddenly she would have been extremely upset. I expect your papa paid her off in lieu of notice and she went on an early train — goodness knows where.'

'She has a sister in London who runs a school so I suppose she'd go there. But why did my father dismiss her? She was very clever so it wasn't anything to do with her teaching.'

'It must have been something else that we don't know about.'

'Perhaps she stole something.'

'No, I don't think it was that.'

'What should I do?'

'I think we'd both better go downstairs and have a word with your uncle. He ought to know about this.'

Ambrose was reading a letter he had found on the desk in his study. He handed it to me with a puzzled expression.

'Nicholas left early before breakfast, which isn't unusual, but I thought he was going to stay with us a little longer after poor Lucy's accident.'

The letter, which was no more than a hasty scrawl, stated Nicholas's intention of leaving very early to catch the seven o'clock train from Bromsley to Birmingham. He had dismissed the governess for insolent behaviour and he was taking her and her luggage to the station in the gig. One of the servants could fetch it back later. Odd conduct, I thought, but Nicholas was nothing if not erratic.

'What on earth can Miss Carr have done to merit instant dismissal?' Ambrose wondered aloud.

'I think I can guess,' I said, 'but Alice is anxious to know what she should do.'

'Have a holiday until we have decided what her future is to be. Will that suit you, Alice?'

'Oh yes!' Her pinched little face brightened and she actually smiled.

'There you are,' I said. 'We'll go for a walk later as I think the rain is giving over. In the meantime go and do your piano practice and I'll come up and fetch you when it's time to go out.'

As she left the room I turned to Ambrose and spoke quietly. 'I believe your brother discovered that Miss Carr had something to do with my sister falling downstairs.'

'He thinks she pushed her?'

'Rather more than thinking, I imagine.'

'But why would Miss Carr do such a wicked thing?'

I knew the answer was jealousy, but I said nothing. Ambrose was obviously ignorant of the affair that had been going on between Nicholas and the governess. It was no business of mine to disillusion him.

'I wonder . . . ' he said, 'if my brother agrees, do you think you could take over as Alice's governess until we find a suitable replacement? The child seems to have taken to you and I'm sure you'd be a very good teacher. It would be a temporary arrangement unless it worked out so well that you would agree to stay on. You'd remain a guest here just as now but I insist on your being paid more than Miss Carr and I believe she received thirty pounds per annum, which was the highest salary any governess could expect. However, you'd be doing it as a favour to the family and giving up your time to help us. You'd be treated as a friend, not an employee.'

'I'm not sure your brother would be happy with the idea.'

'He isn't here most of the time and I'm at a loss what to do with the child. He's never been keen on the idea of a school. Just tell me you'll consider the proposition. You needn't give me an answer now.'

'Yes, I will certainly consider it but it all depends on what your brother decides. You know he doesn't like me.'

'I can't think why, apart from this idiotic notion of your interfering, which you once mentioned. I know Alice is his daughter but she's living in my house and under my unofficial guardianship, at least during the week. He can scarcely object, especially if I offer to provide the necessary remuneration.'

I went away wondering what I was being drawn into. Although I had hoped to get away from Avalon Castle in the near future two things urged me to stay: Lucy needed me at present and then . . . I hardly dared to admit it, but I was looking forward to the spring and William Norton's return from Italy. Now came this third inducement. I liked Alice and I fancied she liked me. I had no experience of teaching, apart from a little tutoring I gave Lucy years ago, but I knew enough music, French, arithmetic and other subjects to instruct an eight-year-old. It would not be an arduous commitment; I would not be treated like a governess and the salary would be useful.

I went to my sister's room, where she lay, as before, propped up on pillows, still looking pale and haggard as she picked at her breakfast.

'She needs building up,' said Mattie, who was in attendance as usual. 'Beef tea and an egg beaten up in milk with a tot of sherry.'

Lucy pulled a face.

'Did you know Miss Carr had been dismissed?' I enquired.

'Really?' Lucy brightened. 'I'm glad to hear it. When is she going?'

'She's already gone.'

'Good riddance to bad rubbish!' muttered Mattie.

'Your husband left early this morning,' I said. 'I thought he was going to stay longer.'

'So did I, but there are problems with the business. He can see I'm going on well and he didn't want to disturb me so he left a note pinned to my pillow telling me he was leaving early.'

Mattie sniffed as she always did when she disapproved of something but thought it was the wrong time to express an opinion. Later, out of Lucy's hearing, I asked her what she was thinking.

'There was something going on last night. I could hear them at it hammer and tongs.'

'Nicholas and Miss Carr?'

'Who else? Of course, I couldn't hear much of it despite holding a glass against the wall, but some of it came through, especially when they shouted — and they did a lot of that.

'I heard him say, 'You've gone too far this time!' Then she shrieked at him but I couldn't catch the words and he shouted back. Then they lowered their voices. I suppose they were afraid of being overheard. This went on for a while, and then there were some peculiar noises and the door opened and closed. A little later there was dragging and thumping. I think she was drawing her trunk across the floor and throwing stuff into it. I got tired then and went to bed but I suppose Mr Nicholas took her off to the station with him before breakfast.'

'Yes, he left a note for his brother.' I said no more but I felt a little uneasy. Something — I scarcely knew what — didn't seem right.

I returned to my own room to put on outdoor clothes and then made my way to the schoolroom where I could hear Alice dutifully practising her scales. The door to Miss Carr's room was open and I could hear female voices engaged in some indignant discussion. I peered inside and found two of the housemaids stripping the bed and folding up the pillow-cases and blankets.

'Is anything the matter?' I enquired.

'Not really, miss, but there's something strange. We were told to tidy the room and remove all the bedding but the sheets are missing — both of them.'

'I reckon she helped herself,' her companion suggested with a knowing look. 'Her way of getting her own back — shoved two good sheets into that great trunk of hers.'

The other girl shrugged. 'Nothing to do with us. What do we do with those books she left? Do you suppose she'll be sending for them, Miss Garland?'

'I've no idea. Perhaps you'd better take them into the schoolroom and I'll have a look at them.'

I went next door and told Alice to prepare for her walk. She remarked on the maids clearing Miss Carr's room, but only to suggest they had wasted no time in ridding the house of her presence.

As we left the house and took the path by the lake we saw, to our surprise, that the two vessels from the boathouse were floating on the water. Two men were in one, trying to secure the other to some sort of tow rope.

Joe Hicks the stable boy ran past us to join them and I called him back.

'What's going on? Do you know why the boats are out today?'

'Nobody knows, miss. It's a mystery. The boathouse was found unlocked this morning and one of the boats was floating on the lake. They've gone out to bring it back.'

'So you don't know who's responsible?'

'Mr Garner' — he named the head groom — 'says somebody broke in to see if there was anything worth stealing and when he found there wasn't, he shoved one of the boats out just to cause trouble. The lock hadn't been forced — that's the odd thing — but there was no sign of the key.'

Joe grinned; he was obviously enjoying the excitement. He had been the Lord of Misrule at Ambrose's ill-fated party.

'I expect you are up very early every day,' I remarked casually.

'Oh yes, miss, half-past five usually.'

'And that was the time you were up this morning? It must have been dark.'

'It always is except in summer, but that doesn't bother me.'

'Did you see Mr Nicholas Blackwood leaving?'

'He always leaves early but he was half an hour earlier and woke me up. I sleep over the stables, miss, and he shouted and banged on the ceiling with a stick. I helped him get the gig ready. He said he was taking Miss Carr to the station with him as she was leaving.'

'Did you see her?'

He shook his head. 'We took the gig to the side door. Mr Nicholas said she was sheltering from the rain inside the vestibule. I helped put her trunk in the gig. It was heavy but there were all her clothes and books inside. Then he dismissed me so I didn't see them leave.'

I was little the wiser but I did not pursue the matter.

With Miss Carr and Nicholas both absent the atmosphere lightened considerably. Dr Sawyer declared Lucy to be quite out of danger and recommended rest and nourishing food together with a tonic of his own devising.

My position as temporary governess to Alice was confirmed. Nicholas, as I expected, was not overanxious for my stay at Avalon to be prolonged but he plainly did not want to bother advertising for another governess. He observed that my teaching duties would keep me fully occupied and I supposed he thought it would give me less time for the prying and interfering he suspected I was doing.

The weeks passed quietly enough, marked by ice and snow and then gradually improving weather. Lucy rallied and moved from her bed to the chaise longue in her boudoir. Then she began to come downstairs again and life returned to normal.

I quite enjoyed teaching Alice, who was an intelligent and diligent child. My position was much superior to that of the usual sort of governess as I did not suffer the isolation and condescension the occupation normally entails. It was not at all onerous and I reflected that I was repaying Ambrose's hospitality.

Towards the end of March, a great upheaval took place which ultimately led to disaster.

14

One afternoon, on my return from an afternoon drive with Lucy, we were greeted by Ambrose in the entrance hall. He was beaming cheerfully and I thought how well he looked: there was colour in his usually pale cheeks and a sparkle in his eye that I had not seen before.

'My dear Rachel and Lucy, we've had such a delightful surprise — the Nortons are home before we expected them. Do come into the great hall and meet the Contessa d'Ortoli.'

I am not sure what I expected: a pale, melancholy figure in widow's weeds, I suppose. Helena d'Ortoli sat in a high-backed chair by the fireplace. Out of the corner of my eye I saw her brother, leaning on a heavy oak table nearby.

She was a very beautiful woman. Even sitting down I could see that she was tall, with an elegant figure. Her hair was deep gold, the colour of corn, her face classical in its proportions yet animated and expressive. She wore blue, not black, perhaps to emphasize the vivid colour of her eyes.

Introductions were made and I found

myself liking her at once. Her manner was so pleasant, so easy and unaffected, that I was reminded of her brother and told her so.

'William? Do you think so? He's supposed to be more like Papa, whereas I'm supposed to take after our mother.'

'She got the brains and I got the beauty,' observed William Norton.

'Imbecile!' she laughed. 'Never take any notice of anything he says.'

'It must be a great upheaval, coming back to England after so many years,' I said.

'Yes and no. At the moment it seems like a holiday. I intend to stay for quite a long time but I am not sure yet whether it will be forever. I love Italy and I may find myself drawn back. I still have a house in Venice which is rented out at present, but I feel it's another home. Perhaps I may divide the year between the two countries. It is too early yet to make up my mind; there are so many things to consider.'

Jessica sat on the other side of the fireplace dispensing tea. She said nothing but glowered at all the company. After pouring out two extra cups for Lucy and me, she sat back with her arms folded and closed her eyes as though deliberately withdrawing from everything that was going on.

I noticed that Lucy, who was equally quiet,

although she attempted to be sociable, was looking fatigued, so I suggested she should go to her room and rest, as she usually did for an hour or two every afternoon.

'Of course you must go,' said Ambrose. 'I'm sure we all excuse you. Dr Sawyer said you must rest as much as possible.'

'Has your sister been unwell?' enquired Mr Norton, when she had gone.

'Yes, quite ill, but she's very much better now and has to be dissuaded from exerting herself too much,' I told him.

'She looks rather delicate,' observed Helena. 'So very pretty and fragile — like a piece of Dresden china.'

'I have so much to tell you,' interposed Ambrose with great enthusiasm. 'I've acquired so many interesting things while you've been away. You must come and see them. You haven't seen the murals since they were completed and there are some glorious tapestries which you'll adore. And then there are the plans for the chapel — you must see those! I can hardly wait to hear your opinion; you always had such excellent taste!'

'Probably ruined by Italy,' she smiled, 'where everything seems to be either over-opulent or exquisitely beautiful.'

'Then come and enjoy a glimpse of the romantic North!'

He held out his hand and she took it, gathering up her billowing blue silk skirts as she rose from the chair.

'Venus rising from the waves!' exclaimed Ambrose in an absurdly sentimental manner as they left the room.

'I'm afraid he's smitten all over again,' sighed William Norton. 'I doubt if their conversation will be confined to fan vaulting and stained glass. She's quite incorrigible; she can't resist exerting her charms on every man in sight. She means no harm; she thrives on affection and admiration but I'm afraid poor Ambrose may be hurt again. Before she went to Italy everyone thought they were on the verge of being engaged, although she did express uncertainties. The separation was intended to help her decide — with the results you know.'

'Yes, I'd heard that was the reason he'd never married.'

'Don't misunderstand me. I'm very fond of both Ambrose and my sister but I can't imagine Helena spending the rest of her life with him. She's never shared my love of the country — not for more than a few weeks anyway. She finds Ambrose's fads and fancies entertaining, but no more. She doesn't share them.

'Anyway, enough of that subject. The two

of them are old enough to look after themselves. How are you? You look very well.'

'Oh, I'm never ill. It's Lucy that's had a problem with her health. I think you should know the details — you're bound to hear something sooner or later and I wouldn't like you to be misled.'

I hastily told him of Lucy's fall downstairs and its consequences. I explained that Miss Carr was the obvious miscreant, especially as Alice and I had discovered the 'bridal' costume at the back of the wardrobe.

'So Nicholas dismissed her instantly?'

'Oh yes, she packed her things and he conveyed her to the railway station at an early hour the next morning. I have my own suspicions as to the motive for her behaviour.'

'Do you think there was something going on between Nicholas and her?'

'I'm afraid so.'

'That doesn't surprise me. It wouldn't be the first time he's stepped out of line. He has a weakness for the fair sex.'

'Lucy doesn't suspect; she is rather naive, you know. She worships Nicholas and won't hear a word against him.'

'But you are still here and she has your help and support, which she must need at present. I'm so glad you've not gone away — and not just because of that.'

'I am now Alice's governess, albeit in a temporary position. I'm not at all sure I'd care to live here permanently.'

'That's understandable. It must be like living in a mausoleum.'

He took both my hands in his. I glanced sideways at Jessica and in a split second caught her squinting at us through one half-opened eye which she shut immediately. Whether she had just woken up or whether she had been listening to our conversation from the first, there was no way of telling.

As he attempted to draw me closer I disengaged myself and nodded towards Jessica.

'Not now,' I whispered.

'Then some time later, I hope. I haven't forgotten the hope I expressed on Christmas Eve. Do you remember?'

'I shan't ever forget.'

'I'm glad to hear it. Now let us sit sedately on the sofa and I'll tell you about my trip to Italy.'

Ambrose and Helena rejoined us nearly an hour later. Jessica had long since 'woken up' and poured more tea but still had little to say apart from expressing her disapproval of foreign places, people, food and behaviour.

'And I don't know why my brother is showing plans of a chapel to your sister, Mr

Norton. What use that will be, I should like to know. He hasn't shown them to Nicholas yet. In fact, he hasn't dared to mention the subject to him, but he'll have to soon if he means to start building. What a waste of money! Some use my saving him pounds by careful management of the household when he throws it all away on fal-lals.' She subsided into grumbles.

When her brother returned with his admired guest she muttered something about hoping they had enjoyed themselves.

'Oh yes,' said Helena brightly. 'It's quite like old times.'

'That's what I was afraid of,' mumbled Jessica.

15

The next couple of weeks passed pleasantly enough. The Nortons dined at Avalon Castle and we dined at Monkstone. There was much coming and going between the two houses and Ambrose seemed exhilarated; his usual dreamy expression was replaced by an animation and intensity I had only previously observed when he was possessed by enthusiasm for his house and its contents.

'I think Ambrose is in love with Helena,' said Lucy. 'But then, he always has been, hasn't he? Do you think he'll marry her this time?'

'It's far too soon to say. We don't know how she feels about him, and anyway, she's only been a widow for a year.'

'She's out of black. One would expect half-mourning at least. Jessica says it's shocking but perhaps she thinks no one in England will know when her husband died. I doubt if she cared much for him.'

'He was a great deal older, I believe, and she's still young. We must make allowances.'

'Do you like her?'

'Yes, I've no reason *not* to like her. She's

very pleasant and unaffected. One might expect a contessa to put on airs and graces but she doesn't. She's open and cheerful and like a breath of fresh air in this house.'

'Nicholas doesn't like her — have you noticed?'

The previous weekend I had observed, when the Nortons dined with us, that Nicholas was rather cool towards Helena and avoided speaking to her except in the most formal manner.

'Yes,' I said, 'there's probably a reason for it.'

'He told me they quarrelled before she went to Italy. He thought she'd treated Ambrose very badly — that she'd led him on and then turned down his proposal. He's afraid the same thing may happen again.'

I did not think Nicholas was so concerned about his brother's welfare but I could not see him welcoming Helena as his sister-in-law. If Ambrose married and had a son there would be an heir to Avalon Castle and half the Blackwoods' business.

Ever since I had taken over the position of governess to Alice we found that Lucy was on much better terms with the child. I wondered if Miss Carr had somehow poisoned her mind against her stepmother. Now, however, Alice was quite happy when Lucy offered to take over her drawing lessons as she was a far better artist than I.

It so happened, therefore, that I had a free afternoon, and as the day was mild and sunny I decided to walk to Monkstone. I suppose at the back of my mind was the hope that I might encounter William Norton. Before our friendship developed into something closer I had to unburden myself regarding my early acquaintance with Nicholas Blackwood.

When I entered the little wood near Monkstone village I heard a dog barking. A few minutes later the Newfoundland Nero came bounding through the undergrowth and I was subjected to a hairy, tail-waving greeting.

'Miss Garland!' cried a voice. 'I was just on my way over to the castle in the hope that I might see you.'

'And I was coming to Monkstone in the hope of seeing you!'

'Happy coincidence! Or have we started reading each other's minds?'

'I don't know, but I am very glad to see you, Mr Norton. There is something I think you ought to know.'

'Then you shall tell me by all means, but as we are so near our first meeting place I think we should revisit it.'

I did not ask why but accompanied him

only too willingly in the direction of the rustic bridge. Once I stumbled over some unevenness in the path and he caught me in his arms. For a few seconds we were in an embrace and I told myself it was my stupid fancy that made me imagine that he held me a little longer and closer than was necessary to preserve my balance.

The last time I had been in that wood it had been winter but now it was spring, with daffodils pushing through the grass. He motioned me to be quiet as we moved onto the bridge.

'Let us wait here for a few minutes. We can talk quietly but don't make any sudden movements. Ah — there — look!' He seized my arm and pointed down the stream. There was a flash of iridescent blue in the sun and then —

Forever afterwards the three things were mingled together in my memory: the slanting beam of sunlight, the kingfisher's flight and the kiss. It was different from the gentle kiss he had given me under the mistletoe and I found myself responding eagerly.

'My dear girl!' he said at last. 'I've been longing to do that ever since I fished you out of the stream, all wet and dishevelled.'

'You caught me off guard,' I said, rather breathlessly.

'Do you mean that if you were *on* guard you wouldn't have allowed such a liberty?'

I laughed. 'I didn't say that.'

'Then I give you warning. I'm going to kiss you again. Now you are quite free to scream, swoon, run away or box my ears. No? Well, this time you can't say you were taken by surprise.'

The second kiss was, I think, even more satisfactory than the first, and then we stood in a comfortable embrace, saying very little. For the first time since I came to Avalon Castle I felt entirely secure. Yet it was not a dull, empty security; the future offered a promise of real happiness.

Then I realized that I could not let our courtship — if that's what it was — proceed if there were any secrets between us. I could not leave him in ignorance any longer. His head bent down again and this time I put my hand over his mouth and he kissed my fingers.

'No — please — no more until I have told you something that has been troubling me — something you ought to know.'

I hastily explained how, back in Northgate, Nicholas Blackwood had made advances in the hope of securing my non-existent fortune, then when he learnt the truth, he transferred his supposed affections to Lucy.

'So you see why I mistrusted him from the

first,' I said. 'He has married Lucy for her money and would have been quite happy to accept me had our fortunes been reversed.'

'His conduct does not surprise me. He has always been ruthless as far as money is concerned. But what were your feelings towards him? If he'd proposed marriage would you have accepted?'

'To be perfectly honest I don't know. I'd not had any experience of marriage proposals. I would certainly have suggested that we should wait a while and get to know each other better.' I hesitated. 'I don't think I altogether trusted him even then. There was something about him that made me feel uneasy, but I did find him strangely attractive. That's quite gone. From the moment he eloped with Lucy I loathed him. I think he's perfectly heartless and mercenary.'

'You are probably right and I think you have acted quite properly. The circumstances are extraordinary and you must certainly be anxious for your sister's welfare. But at least you have a friend in me. You can run over to Monkstone if the situation ever becomes intolerable. I'll do anything in my power to help you.'

We were still pressed close together, his arm around my shoulders, when Helena came upon us, walking through the wood on the way to Avalon Castle, or so I assumed.

'Lovely afternoon, Helena!' he observed cheerfully, making no attempt to release me.

'We've just seen a kingfisher.'

'How exciting! And not the only interesting activity by the look of it.' There was something sardonic in both her voice and her look but I was too dazed with happiness to take much notice of it.

'Off to Avalon?' enquired William. 'Don't play 'La Belle Dame Sans Merci' with poor Ambrose. He's suffered enough.'

'Oh, I'll do my best to be merciful, you can be sure of that!' The Contessa said no more but smiled a little and bestowed on us a curious glance, half calculating, half satirical, before going on her way.

'I shouldn't be surprised if Helena gets an offer soon,' said William, as we strolled along with his arm around my waist.

'But she's only been back a few weeks.'

'And they've seven years to bridge in that time. They are both older and, I hope, wiser than before.'

'Then you think she'll accept?'

'Ah now, I didn't say that. I'm not at all sure they'd be happy. Ambrose adores her; he always did. And she is very fond of him, although he exasperates her at times. Helena is a very down-to-earth person, you know, and dear old Ambrose is always lost in a dream, but I'd be happy enough to have him as a brother-in-law. He's perfectly eligible and at least I'd have her as my neighbour.'

I thought, for a moment, of the disruption to the household at Avalon Castle if Ambrose did indeed marry Helena. She was not a gentle, inexperienced girl but a widow of rank with a determined character, used to giving orders. Jessica might not welcome her authority and would Helena want to share her house with the rest of Ambrose's family? I had once heard her declare that the whole place needed 'brightening up'.

'You look very thoughtful,' my companion observed.

'I was just speculating on the future if they do marry.'

'I'm pretty sure he hasn't asked her yet or she'd have told me. After what happened last time he'll probably want to be more certain of the result. It may take a man a little while to summon up the resolution, however he may feel in his own mind. Dear Rachel, can you wait a little?'

'Wait? For what?'

'For a clod like me to sort himself out.'

'Why yes, though I'm not quite sure what you mean.'

'You must know by now that I can't make

134

fine speeches or act like someone out of a novel. Even if I tried we'd both probably laugh at me. Be patient, my dear, and for the present we'll simply enjoy each other's company.'

On my return to Avalon Castle, my head full of agreeable fantasies and feeling happier than at any time since my sister's marriage, I was brought abruptly back to earth by men's voices raised in violent argument.

16

The library door to the left of the entrance hall stood open and Nicholas's bellowing was perfectly audible, as was the gentler voice of Ambrose, which sounded louder and harder than usual.

'Preposterous notions!' cried Nicholas Blackwood. 'A chapel indeed! And an organ! For you to say your prayers in suitable splendour and play those insipid melodies of yours. No doubt it will be grander than anything the Queen might own. You must be insane! You've always been eccentric and now you've toppled into madness. Where's the money coming from, I'd like to know?'

'What I do with my share of the profits is my affair.'

'Oh indeed! Then let me tell you, since you're so ill-informed and so little interested in the business, that we'll be lucky to have any profits this year, the way things are going.'

'You've been saying that for as long as I can remember.'

'It happens to be true. The whole arms trade has slumped since the end of the

American war. You've thrown away every penny on this place instead of reinvesting. I wanted to branch out into other industries but you wouldn't hear of it. All Lucy's money has been swallowed up. Now look where we are — on the edge of bankruptcy.'

'Nonsense!' snapped Ambrose. 'You always think you can override me by shouting exaggerated complaints about the state of the business.'

'They are not exaggerated and I could very well object to the furtive way you've gone about this latest lunacy — having plans drawn up behind my back.'

'That is a gross distortion!'

I had heard enough, fascinating as I found it, so I crept through the entrance hall, deciding it would be far too embarrassing to encounter the two angry men. I went through the hall into the courtyard, crossed to the door near the morning room and, having avoided one awkward situation, walked straight into another.

Helena d'Ortoli was sitting on the sofa, surrounded by swatches of velvet and brocade. She looked up with a smile as I entered.

'Ah, so you've torn yourself away from my dear brother! I'm just trying to choose some new curtains for this room. I've told Ambrose that these dreary things will not do at all. Grey-blue serge — really! They've faded dreadfully and look so drab and dusty. I've narrowed the choice down to two. Which do you prefer? The pale-yellow damask or the crimson velvet?'

'The red, I think.'

'Mm! I prefer the yellow after all. However, I'm sure Ambrose will have the final word. Did you enjoy your visit to Monkstone?'

The change of subject was disconcerting, which was no doubt her intention.

'Very much,' I said, quite truthfully.

'William can be very agreeable, as many young ladies have found out to their cost, but he is not to be taken seriously. He *will* flirt, though there are few opportunities in the country. It really is too bad of him; he ought to have more regard for other people's feelings but he's never had much imagination. He looks so amiable, that's the trouble; no one would expect him of being a heart-breaker. And as for my poor friend, Catherine Lester, she cannot pin him down to a positive date for the wedding, though after such a long engagement I'd have thought there was no point in waiting further. I know there was that long delay when her father was so ill and then William came to me in Italy, but there's now really nothing to stand in their way.'

'Your brother is engaged to be married?'

'Ah, I don't suppose he told you; Catherine is my oldest and closest friend. She lives in Worcester.'

She went on talking but I heard no more. It was as though the light of the day had been extinguished. I tried to smile and hide my feelings but I could not trust myself to say much more and quickly made the excuse that I must see my sister and my pupil, whose drawing lesson would now be at an end. In the corridor leading to the stairs I met Jessica Blackwood, who was looking even more disgruntled than usual.

'Still in the morning room, is she?'

'The Contessa? Yes, she's looking at curtain materials.'

Jessica sniffed. 'What business it is of hers I can't imagine. The present ones are quite serviceable. She takes too much upon herself.'

'Your brothers seem to be having some sort of disagreement in the library,' I said. 'I couldn't help hearing part of it as I was passing through the hall, their voices were so loud. It was about the proposed chapel, I think.'

'Oh, *that*!' Jessica sniffed again. 'I knew Nicholas would be against it but Ambrose will have his way. Once he's set his mind on something he can be very stubborn. It's nothing for you to worry about.'

'I'm not worried. I just thought you'd like to know.'

She shrugged. 'It was only to be expected.'

I went to my room, not much caring what Lucy and Alice might be doing. I told myself I had presumed too much. In the beginning I had told myself that I could expect no more than friendship with William Norton. I had been a fool to let myself hope. And yet — he did not seem to me the sort of man who would amuse himself by flirting with every available woman. But he had made a curious remark which I had not understood at the time: *Can you wait a little, for a clod like me to sort himself out?*

Had the kisses been a mere impulse without any real meaning?

I wished I could find solace in tears but I had learnt not to cry easily and so it hurt more to bear the dreary weight of disappointment without relief. Perhaps I was in danger of indulging in self-pity but such thoughts were pushed aside when Lucy came looking for me.

'Alice has done very well and wants to show you her pictures,' she said. 'Where's Nicholas? He was at lunch but I haven't seen him since.'

'He's still in the library as far as I know, having a quarrel with Ambrose about his plans for a chapel.'

'I do think Ambrose is taking things too far. Nicholas says the business is not doing well and we must be careful about expenditure. He was hoping originally to buy us a nice house in the Birmingham suburbs where we could be on our own but he's having to economize.'

'You had enough money to buy a substantial property and have plenty left over for living expenses.'

'I don't think we can count on that any more.' She looked troubled. 'It would be nice to have my own home and furnish it the way I want and my own servants and a carriage. I don't like relying on Ambrose, kind as he is. What will happen if he marries Helena d'Ortoli? He seems very devoted to her.'

'Yes, I believe he is, though whether his feelings are reciprocated to the same extent I wouldn't care to say.'

'She seems quite charming and she's certainly beautiful.'

I nodded but I was beginning to wonder if the Contessa was quite as agreeable as I had thought at first.

'I don't think your husband would approve of the match,' I said.

'Oh, no! I told you how much he dislikes her. It would be a great upheaval here if she married Ambrose. I'm not sure I'd want to stay on even if she invited me. Staying with a bachelor brother-in-law is not at all the same as living with a newly married couple, even in a house the size of this. What would you do?'

'I have no idea. I don't think Alice would be very happy about the situation.'

'I'm sure you'd be able to stay on as her governess.'

'Perhaps, but I don't know if I'd want to. I've a feeling I would no longer be considered a family member and I have no wish to be the sort of governess who is treated with condescension and takes all her meals in the schoolroom.'

'I hope you'll always be near to me, whatever is decided.'

'Not if it involves living in Birmingham.'

'Oh dear, I almost hope the romance comes to nothing, even though I wouldn't like Ambrose to be hurt. I really am very fond of him.'

I accompanied her back to the schoolroom where Alice proudly exhibited her pictures.

'Do you think Uncle Ambrose is going to marry the Contessa?' she asked, when I had duly admired her work.

'That's not for us to decide,' I said wearily.

'I've seen them holding hands and he put his arm round her waist when they were walking in the garden. Does that mean he's in love with her?'

'Not necessarily. They've known each other a very long time and I'm sure they're very fond of each other. That's not always the same as being in love.'

But that evening at dinner Helena had stayed on to join us and she was sporting a fine diamond ring on her right hand.

'Look what Ambrose has given me!' she declared. 'It was his mother's so it's of great sentimental value. I have yet to decide whether to transfer it to my wedding finger because then it becomes an engagement ring with all that implies.'

'I want you to keep the ring, whatever you decide,' said Ambrose earnestly. 'No one else will ever wear it.'

Nicholas glared at her with undisguised hostility.

Alice and I encountered him the next morning as we took our morning walk. He was striding along one of the paths towards the house, hatless with his hair dishevelled and a rather flushed, abstracted look.

'Papa!' cried Alice, running towards him. 'I see so little of you when you are here. Please stay with us a while.'

He embraced her in a perfunctory fashion. 'I can't do that, I'm afraid, my dear. You must know I'm a very busy man and have to work hard even when I come here for the weekend.'

'But you've been out now.'

'I need a breath of air at times. Now I must go in and look over the accounts I brought with me.'

He acknowledged my presence with a brusque nod and then went on his way.

'I wonder if he would have loved me more if I'd been a boy,' she said sadly.

'It's just his manner. He's like that with everybody,' I said soothingly, but I felt annoyed by his treatment of the child. He seemed hardly aware of her existence.

'Could we go over to Monkstone?' she asked. 'We might meet Mr Norton and his lovely dog or see that kingfisher you told me about.'

'It's Sunday,' I reminded her. 'There isn't time before church.'

'This afternoon then — or tomorrow . . . '

That was the last thing I wanted and I managed to dissuade her by presenting her with an agreeable alternative. Mr Norton was the last person on earth I wished to meet.

17

The next week passed quietly enough. Lucy observed that I seemed in low spirits. I told her nothing but made some excuse about the weather, which had turned wet and blustery and kept us indoors. When William Norton and his sister came to dinner I took a meal in the nursery with Alice. When we were invited to dine at Monkstone I declined to accompany the others. I received a letter which I returned unopened.

At the weekend Nicholas Blackwood did not come to Avalon Castle but stayed in town. Ambrose seemed rather relieved. He was constantly in the company of Helena d'Ortoli. She came every day from Monkstone, taking William's shabby old carriage if the weather was inclement but otherwise walking or riding. She looked very well in her black habit, worn with a rather masculine hat with a veil.

Ambrose and Helena spent many hours alone together in the library, or, in the few sunny intervals, strolling outside in the park. Once Alice claimed to have seen them kissing but the diamond ring remained on

Helena's right hand.

The next weekend Nicholas arrived as usual but the brothers still seemed on frosty terms. After dinner Ambrose said he had one of his blinding headaches. He had certainly looked ill all through the meal and ate nothing. I could not help wondering how much the arrival of Nicholas had contributed to his indisposition. Helena, who had been at Avalon all day, as was usual now, said she would accompany him to the door of his room in case he felt faint. She returned a little later saying Ambrose was going to take a dose of laudanum before retiring.

'I thought he'd already had one but he usually knows how much to take,' she said, and took her leave shortly afterwards.

Early next morning when I was up and dressed but had not yet done my hair, I was surprised to hear someone singing below my window. It was a baritone voice attempting, none too successfully, a tenor aria.

'*La donna è mobile*
Qual piuma al vento
Muta d'accento
E di pensier . . . '

At this point whistling continued the tune. None of the servants could be singing in

Italian, nor did the sound diminish as though they were walking by. Whoever was below remained there. I went to the open window and looked down. William stood on the terrace looking up at me with his usual cheerful expression. He doffed his hat.

'Good morning, Rachel. I hope you appreciate my serenade.'

'You should attempt something within your range.'

'Ah, but I chose that aria on account of the words. Are you familiar with their English meaning?'

'Really, Mr Norton, I have other things to do than — '

'Your continual excuse at the moment. I think I am entitled to a few minutes of your time, especially as you look so fetching with your hair loose.'

I ought to have closed the window and moved away but the attraction of his presence was too much for me. However painful, I had to stay, thinking that at least he owed me an apology, and an explanation.

'Woman is fickle!' I said.

'Like a feather wafted,' he continued, 'changeable in action and in thought.'

'*You* think *me* fickle, Mr Norton? I'd have thought you were more deserving of that adjective.'

'May I ask why? Or will you do me the honour to come down and talk to me? I think if you have anything to discuss I'd sooner hear it outright. But we cannot talk privately like this. I'll wait in the summerhouse by the lake.'

There I joined him ten minutes later. It was an interview I dreaded, yet there was a kind of relief in bringing it all out into the open. He smiled and held out his arms to me but seeing me stand, frozen and unhappy, his expression changed.

'My dear Rachel,' he said gently. 'What *is* the matter?'

'Well may you ask! A certain lady in Worcester is the matter.'

'A certain lady? Ah, has Helena said anything to you?'

'How else could I be expected to know? You were not exactly forthcoming.'

'Perhaps you'll let me know precisely what my sister told you.'

I repeated her words as nearly as I could recall them.

'I see. Now please let me explain. It is true I was once engaged to the young lady in question. It was years ago, before Helena was married. She and Catherine Lester were at school together and often stayed with each other. It was natural that Catherine and I

148

should drift into a romantic attachment. Neither of us at that time had much opportunity for mixing with members of the opposite sex. After a year she broke it off. Her parents had married late; her mother was forty when she was born and her father was much older. He was in poor health and she was needed at home. I think, however, that was a convenient excuse, as we had both begun to realize that we had nothing in common. She loved the town, I preferred the country. She loved music, dancing, company; I loved peace and quiet. She detested horses and disliked dogs.'

'Then your sister deliberately misled me when she suggested the engagement had continued?'

'Put bluntly, she lied to you. No — there's no need to soften it. I can't excuse her. Helena can be difficult at times; it comes of always having her own way. When matters are not to her liking she tries to push them into a shape she fancies better. She always wanted me to marry Catherine Lester and would never accept our betrothal had come to an end. I always hoped Catherine would marry someone else, because as long as she remained single Helena would continue to hope. Miss Lester is very eligible. Not, perhaps, very intelligent, but pretty and lively and, as she's an only child, likely to inherit a good fortune.'

'I'm surprised she hasn't got a long line of suitors waiting at her door.'

'Perhaps she has. I haven't seen her for years. I don't even know if she and Helena have corresponded in the interim.'

'Mr Norton — '

'Oh please call me William — or Bill if you prefer it. I can no longer think of you as Miss Garland.'

'Very well, but I'm not quite sure we can go back. Last time we spoke you said something rather strange.'

'Did I?'

'You said something about waiting a little until you'd sorted yourself out.'

'That meant nothing in particular. I have started thinking seriously of marriage and all that it implies. I would like to see Helena settled one way or the other before I share my home with a wife. I know you must feel distressed. I'm sorry with all my heart that you were given such an unfortunate impression of my conduct.'

'Your sister must think me a very poor substitute for Miss Lester. I am surprised you consider me to be in any way suited to be her successor.'

'Are you really? Don't you realize, you silly

girl, that I have enjoyed every moment I have spent in your company and if I lived with you for fifty years, I don't think I could ever tire of it?'

He spoke with such warm simplicity and sincerity that I was moved. I could not help but believe him, and, seeing some softening of my expression, he took my hands in his.

'Let us start our friendship again as we began it — by water. I shall not keep you too long from your breakfast. Do you realize that is the only meal we have never shared? Luncheon, tea and dinner, yes, but not breakfast. I wonder . . . there is a table here in the summerhouse, and chairs, and it is a beautiful morning. Do you think we might share a pot of tea and some toast? Wait here and I'll see what I can find.'

He ran back to the house and I sat down on the bench outside the summerhouse. The spring day was bright with sunlight and birdsong and again I was full of hope for the future. I felt so much happier than when I set out, yet there remained a trace of disillusionment. Now I realized that Helena d'Ortoli, whom I had liked so much initially, had deceived me and was not to be trusted.

William arrived presently followed by a maid with a tray and I was just pouring the tea when we saw Mattie hastening round the edge of the lake towards us. We stood up as she approached and went forward to meet her. She was flushed beetroot-red and so out of breath she could hardly speak.

'You'd better come quick,' she gasped. 'Something terrible's happened.'

'Calm down and get your breath back,' said William.

'No time, sir — you must come straight away. Something's happened to Mr Ambrose. He's locked in his room and Miss Blackwood sent the stable boy up a ladder to look in and he's sitting in a chair not moving even though the lad beat on the window. They're afraid he's dead!'

18

We hurried back to the house, Mattie stumbling behind us. On going upstairs we found Jessica and several of the servants standing outside the door of Ambrose's room.

'Shall I try and force the door?' enquired William.

'No, Nicholas has gone for the spare key. I don't carry the keys to the bedrooms. There are too many.' Her face was extremely grim but she seemed determined not to let her emotions show. Sometimes I wondered if she had any.

Nicholas arrived at last with the key. 'Let's hope this works,' he said. 'If he's left his key on the other side we may have problems.'

The door opened easily enough and we entered very quietly, the servants staying outside in the passage. I think we all realized almost immediately that we were in the presence of death.

Ambrose sat in a wing chair, wearing his dressing gown. His head was bent forward, his eyes closed. One arm hung over the side of the chair. On the small table beside him stood a lamp and beside it an open book and a small bottle which lay on its side, empty of its contents.

'He's cold,' said Nicholas, taking his brother's hand, 'and there's no pulse.'

'Try holding a mirror to his mouth,' said Jessica, hovering on the other side of the table.

'No point,' said Nicholas, picking up the empty bottle and examining it.

'That's the laudanum he takes,' said Jessica. 'Nasty stuff! He had a headache last night and went to bed early.'

'Yes,' Nicholas replied. 'I remember Helena going upstairs with him because he seemed unsteady and then coming back and telling us he was going to take a draught before going to bed.'

'But he'd locked the door,' said William, 'so where is the key?'

Nicholas looked about him and then searched the pockets of the dead man's dressing gown.

'Here it is.'

'I can understand his locking the door if he wanted to be undisturbed, but why did he take out the key?' said William. 'It would have made more sense to leave it in the door.'

Nicholas shrugged. 'He wasn't well and he probably wasn't thinking very clearly. He obviously took an overdose by mistake.'

William Norton had picked up the open book. 'Christina Rossetti's poems,' he said, glancing at the spine. 'Read it out for us, Rachel, I'm sure we'd all like to hear the last thing he read before he died.'

I took the book from his hand and began to read, unsteadily at first and then with greater confidence.

'When I am dead, my dearest,
Sing no sad songs for me;
Plant thou no roses at my head
Nor shady cypress tree:
Be the green grass above me
With showers and dewdrops wet;
And if thou wilt, remember,
And if thou wilt, forget.'

'That sounds very like a farewell,' said William. 'Are you sure the overdose was accidental?'

'Of course it was!' exclaimed Nicholas roughly. 'Do you know that nearly a hundred people die every year of laudanum overdose?'

'Nasty stuff! I always thought it was dangerous,' said Jessica. She suddenly snatched the book from my hand. 'I think I'd better have that,' she said, and whisked it away into some mysterious pocket in her skirts.

'You'd better send for your doctor and inform the police,' said William. 'The next few days are likely to be very unpleasant but I'm sure a verdict of accidental death will be brought at the inquest.'

'Inquest?' Jessica almost shouted the word. 'Why an inquest?'

'Because all sudden deaths like this must be followed by an inquest to determine the cause,' said Nicholas. 'There shouldn't be any problems in this case: it's so obviously an accident.'

I could not help but wonder at the composure shown by poor Ambrose's brother and sister. Even William seemed upset and when I remembered the kindness Ambrose had shown me I felt close to tears. At last Nicholas seemed to recall what he should be feeling and patted his dead brother's shoulder.

'Poor old Ambrose, you didn't deserve to go like this. I hope you've gone to the real Avalon.'

'I hope he's gone straight to Heaven, not some imaginary place!' Jessica declared stoutly. 'It's no more than his due. He was a good man for all his strange ideas.'

In the midst of all this tragedy Helena d'Ortoli arrived, having intended to accompany Ambrose to church. She came running upstairs in great agitation, having heard from the servants below that their master had been found dead.

'He can't be *dead*!' she cried, bursting into the room and then abruptly halting at the sight of Ambrose's body.

'But he was perfectly well last night — he complained of a headache and seemed rather drowsy at times but he'd always had migraines.'

'Yes,' said Nicholas. 'I noticed the drowsiness and I'm sure he'd already taken one dose for the pain.'

'I walked upstairs with him to this very door,' she said. 'I thought he seemed a little unsteady and I wanted a quiet word with him. I told him I couldn't agree to marry him yet — it was too soon. He said he understood and as I'd been widowed barely a year it wouldn't be proper anyway. But he asked if he could live in hope and I said yes and he kissed me goodnight in the sweetest way — ' She burst into tears and would have thrown herself on Ambrose's body if her brother had not taken her in his arms and led her from the room.

Lucy had still to be told, although I fancied Mattie had already imparted the sad news. When I reached Lucy's room I found her weeping.

'Oh, Rachel! Poor, poor Ambrose! He was always so kind to me. I felt he was truly my brother. I suppose Nicholas will take over the house now and everything else. Mattie says Helena is here. She must be very shocked.'

'Of course, and I really don't think she has any reason to feel guilty. She hadn't rejected him — just postponed giving him an answer. I'm sure the overdose was an accident.'

'Mattie says the police will have to be involved and there'll be an inquest.'

'I'm afraid so.'

⋆ ⋆ ⋆

Inspector Carver questioned everybody but not at any great length and the general impression given was that the whole thing was a formality. Helena was probably the most inconvenienced and emerged from the inter-view dabbing her eyes, but it was, she presumed, because she was the last to see the deceased alive and could give a description of his demeanour and frame of mind.

The inquest took place two days later at the village inn, though the jury were first brought up to the house to inspect the scene of the tragedy and view the corpse. All went smoothly and far more swiftly than anyone dared to hope. The verdict was accidental death and the coroner delivered a little homily on the dangers of taking laudanum.

It seemed to me that it was Jessica who suffered most, despite her superficial self-control. Once or twice she came close to breaking down and there were times when she stumbled about with reddened eyes, oblivious to everyone as though shut away in her own world of despair. Once I tried to speak to her to express some sympathy but she brushed me aside.

'You mean well,' she said sharply, 'but it can't bring him back. What's done is done and the least said the better. I knew something was going to happen; I felt it in my bones.'

'Better leave her alone,' said a voice behind me as Jessica plodded out of the room. I turned and found Nicholas Blackwood at my elbow.

'I think she's feeling it deeply,' I said. 'I wish I could help in some way.'

'You can't. Nobody can. Ambrose was everything to her.'

'And you?'

'Second best. But now I am King of the Castle, so to speak.'

'Yes, it's worked out very well for you, hasn't it?' Not for the first time I reflected how Ambrose's death had brought every possible advantage to his brother. If Ambrose had married Helena and they'd had children, Avalon Castle would have passed out of Nicholas's reach forever. Ambrose would have continued lavishing money on his extravagant whims, assisted by Helena's legacy. Now everything had come to Nicholas. Many a murder had been done for less . . . I shuddered at the thought.

Instinctively I drew away from him but he suddenly seized my hands in his.

'Come, Rachel, I hope we may be better friends. Remember that now this is my house you are dependent on my good will. Not that I would wish to deprive Lucy of your company or Alice of your instruction.'

'I hope not, indeed.'

'Poor Ambrose, he never did quite belong in this world.'

'No? It is true he lived much in a world of the imagination but it never affected his kindness or his consideration for others — unlike those who live solely for modern money-grabbing.'

He laughed. 'Oh yes, very reprehensible! But Ambrose was an expert at spending the money gained by the hard work of others. I'm thinking of selling this place — it's far too big, too gloomy, too expensive to run. I'd like to buy a more modest and comfortable property near Birmingham.'

'Are you serious?'

'Aren't I always?'

'I don't know. I have given up trying to understand you.'

'I'm a practical man. I'd prefer a house with gas lighting where the kitchen isn't a couple of miles from the dining-room and which is warm in winter. It would be better for Lucy's health.'

'The town better than the country?'

'The suburbs are perfectly healthy and Lucy would have more company and amusement. I haven't told her yet; it won't be for a year or so anyway. It will take a while to clear up Ambrose's will, let alone find a buyer for this sepulchre, so there's no need for you to pack your traps. You seem to be doing very well with Alice. She's quite taken to you.'

'Does Jessica know of your intentions?'

'I'd prefer not to tell her at present; it's too soon after Ambrose's death. I'm sure she'd prefer a house in or near the town: she still thinks of Birmingham as home.'

'Why are you telling me all this? I never thought I was to be your confidante.'

'Ah,' he smiled. 'Whatever our differences may be, I do trust you.'

Which is more than I do you, I thought.

Matters soon took a dramatic turn, however, which changed everything in a totally unexpected way. We had all, I think, taken too much for granted.

19

Ambrose's funeral took place in the village church and he was buried in the graveyard. It was a quiet ceremony, the women returning to the house immediately once the actual service was over. There were a number of curious villagers in attendance who behaved decently. The trouble came afterwards when everyone assembled in the dining-room for the reading of Ambrose's will by Mr Slater, his solicitor from Worcester.

As I was not really a member of the family and not likely to be a beneficiary I had no intention of attending, but a message came that I was to go.

Mr Slater began by explaining that Mr Blackwood had recently made a new will, a fact which he wished to keep secret. He had visited the solicitor's office ostensibly to consult him over a dispute concerning a leasehold property and while there, he had made a new will.

No one said anything but the atmosphere in the room changed perceptibly and I saw Nicholas Blackwood's hand clench into a fist.

The minor bequests to servants and friends

came first. I was surprised to find he had left me two hundred pounds and a picture I had admired as 'a token of friendship'. I was touched; I had not known him really well and the fact that he had thought of me at all showed a kindly and generous nature. Lucy was the recipient of a diamond brooch and bracelet belonging to the Blackwoods' mother.

The tension increased as Mr Slater concluded the first part of the will. He then paused and adjusted his spectacles. I thought he was enjoying himself.

'To my sister Jessica the property known as Kilwood Cottage with adjacent garden, orchard and outbuildings. Also the sum of ten thousand pounds in Consolidated Stock and the silver tea service which belonged to our mother.

'To my niece, Alice Blackwood, the sum of two thousand pounds in Consolidated Stock and the pearl necklace which belonged to her grandmother.

'To my brother Nicholas the watch and chain which belonged to our father and his mahogany bureau.

'The remainder of my property, including Avalon Castle and its park, home farm and other lands pertaining to the estate, is to go to Contessa Helena d'Ortoli — '

'*What?*' Nicholas sprang to his feet with an outraged roar.

'Please be seated, Mr Blackwood, I have not quite finished,' Mr Slater protested mildly.

'This cannot be allowed!'

'I beg your pardon, Mr Blackwood.'

'Ambrose left the house and estate to me.'

'In his previous will he did indeed make that bequest but this will was made last month.'

'I shall contest it. He must have been of unsound mind when he made it.'

'I assure you he was completely rational when he drew up this will and I would state as much in any court of law. I knew your brother for many years and I would certainly have been aware of anything unusual in his mental state. He confided in me the reasons for this change of heart and everything seemed perfectly sensible and carefully thought out.'

'I would like to know what his reasons were,' demanded Nicholas.

'I will inform you later in privacy.'

'That won't do. I want to know now!' Nicholas thumped the table with his fist.

'Very well. Mr Blackwood told me that you and he had a strong difference of opinion concerning certain building projects he had

165

in mind. As he wished the house to go to someone who would appreciate it and as he hoped at that time to marry the Contessa d'Ortoli, he thought it more appropriate that the property should go to her.'

'A man makes a new will *after* he marries, not before!' shouted Nicholas.

'I am well aware of that, Mr Blackwood, but your brother's wishes were clear; he did not want the estate to go to you but to the Contessa, whether he eventually married her or not. It was his to dispose of at any time and in any way he thought fit.'

I looked at Helena, her face flushed but frozen into a sad half-smile. I wondered if she had expected this turn of events. Had Ambrose confided in her or had she simply expected a few items of jewellery and artistic bibelots?

Jessica's arms were folded, her head bowed. Nicholas charged out of the room and Lucy ran after him.

I think I was almost as astonished as my brother-in-law. He had been so sure, so confident, and now all his plans were destroyed. If Nicholas had anything to do with his brother's death, or even if he had simply wished him dead in order to secure his property, then providence had given him a suitable reward. He did, however, inherit

Ambrose's half of the family business, which came to him through the will of their father. It was some compensation perhaps but he had expected so much more. The new Birmingham house would have to come from his own funds.

Helena let it be known that she would not be taking up residence in Avalon Castle in the foreseeable future. It would be some time before probate was granted and she was content to wait.

'You must all continue to think of this place as your home,' she said, 'at least for the time being. I have no wish to turn everyone out. I shall return to Monkstone. After all, I'm not sure I'll ever want to live here. It really is rather a fright, as houses go, isn't it? Poor Ambrose believed it was so beautiful and I never had the heart to tell him what I really thought.'

'It'll take a month of Sundays to clear this place out,' said Jessica grimly.

'Oh, such things can be arranged. Whoever buys the house will probably want the furniture and fittings so it's only personal items that will need to be removed. It will not be for quite a while anyway.'

I thought Nicholas would immediately return to town but he stayed on. Lucy told me that he had many things to do concerning

Ambrose's share of the business. She was vague, of course. Lucy was always vague about 'the business'. Perhaps it was true that there were papers in Ambrose's study which had to be removed but I was suspicious. I saw little of him: a glimpse of his gloomy, scowling face as he passed me in the corridor without a glance, let alone a word; a view of his distant figure stumping about beside the lake. I thought of Napoleon at St Helena and thought that he too might have walked with such a vigorous yet listless gait. He took his meals apart from the rest of us and did not join us in the drawing room. If Helena came over from Monkstone he deliberately avoided her to the extent of leaving any room she entered.

It was a week after the funeral that Lucy fell ill. She did not appear at breakfast, and afterwards, one of the maids brought me a message from Mattie, asking me to go to Lucy's room.

My sister sat, as I had seen her before, in her high wing-chair with a towel held below her chin and a slop pail beside her. She looked very pale and sickly.

I turned to Mattie, who was red-eyed as though she had been crying.

'Is it the same as before?' I asked.

'If you mean is she expecting again, no she

isn't. This is something else. She only had tea and toast for breakfast and very little of that. Not much to be sick on.'

'I shall be all right soon; it's only a bilious attack,' said Lucy, smiling feebly.

'What do you think, Miss Rachel? Ought we to send for the doctor?'

'Oh no, not yet. Everybody has a stomach upset occasionally. If it passes off we needn't worry.'

I wondered if the recent upsets had caused this outcome. Ambrose's death, the prospect of leaving for a new home as yet unknown and the bad temper of her husband seemed enough to make a sensitive creature like Lucy become ill.

'Don't upset yourself, Mattie. I'm sure she'll be well again quite soon.'

'I'm not *that* upset,' she said. 'Not yet anyway, but I've had a shock. I don't want to tell you about it in front of — ' She nodded towards Lucy, who was leaning over the pail again.

'Come into the dressing room for a few minutes,' I suggested, and she followed me in, closing the door all but a crack so that she could keep an eye on Lucy.

'Mr Blackwood sent for me,' she said in a low, tremulous voice. 'He told me my services were no longer required. He said a number of the servants were going to be dismissed and as I'm old and suffer from rheumatism, I ought to retire. Well, I may be over seventy but no one ever suggested I was incapable.'

'Of course you're not, and he had no right to talk to you like that; he's not your employer for a start. Lucy and I pay your wages and we certainly have no intention of dismissing you. In fact, I don't know what we'd do without you.'

'Well, I told him that, more or less. I said I'd worked for the Garland family since Miss Lucy was born and no one had ever found fault with me. I still consider myself a Garland servant, quite separate from the Blackwood household. But there is one thing more, miss.'

'Go on.'

'He said I could go to the devil as far as he was concerned — if you'll pardon the language — but he wouldn't have me anywhere near his wife. I'm afraid, Miss Rachel, that he has the right to decide who attends her.'

'I'll have a word with him and explain the situation. He's very impatient and impulsive and I'm afraid he's been in a bad mood ever since the will was read. Don't worry, Mattie, we'll get this settled.'

I spoke cheerfully but I was not at all sure

Nicholas would change his mind and he was surely within his rights to decide who was caring for his wife.

After luncheon I sought him out and found him in the library surrounded by papers. Our interview was short and unpleasant. As I expected, he accused me of interfering in matters which did not concern me and advised me to mind my own business or I would be 'out on my ear'.

I pointed out that the Contessa d'Ortoli had inherited Avalon Castle and she had assured us all that we could stay on for the time being.

'That woman!' he exclaimed bitterly. 'I wish to God she'd stayed in Italy and married another of their decadent spineless aristocrats. She is nothing but trouble!'

'Yet we are all beholden to her, like it or not,' I said, trying to keep calm. 'Mattie has always been a pillar of strength to our family — totally loyal and trustworthy. She really loves Lucy as though she were her own child.'

'She's too old and fussy and domineering. Lucy needs someone younger, a cheerful maid who understands modern fashions, not a gloomy, dowdy old crone.'

'You are being unkind. And you certainly had no right to tell Mattie she was dismissed. She's not your servant.'

'Perhaps not,' he conceded, 'but that's all the more reason why I don't want her attending my wife. It's up to me to choose the members of my household and when we move to a new home we won't be able to afford a large staff. So keep Meddlesome Mattie away from Lucy; if I find her in our rooms again there'll be trouble.'

'Lucy doesn't know yet. She'll be very upset; she looks on Mattie as a second mother. Besides, she's been quite ill this morning; you know she's not strong.'

'You coddle her — you and that silly old woman. There's nothing the matter with her that a couple of children wouldn't put right. And as for you — I suppose you must realize that you'll no longer be required as governess. I've changed my mind about school for Alice. Now Ambrose has gone and the house is to be sold, I think the sooner she is sent to a decent school the better. She probably won't like it but it will do her good.'

There was no point talking to him any more so I returned to tell Mattie what had transpired.

'You can certainly stay on with me,' I said, 'especially as we'll have to leave this house eventually. I thought we might take a cottage somewhere, not too far from Lucy, wherever she might be.'

172

Mattie nodded. 'At least he's not here all the time. When he's gone back to town I can sneak in and see her.'

I was not sure that was going to be so easy, especially when I found out who had been appointed in Mattie's place: a smart, pert housemaid called Lizzie Fox. Although she was not a trained lady's maid, she was quick to learn and pointed out rather saucily that Mattie was not a lady's maid either.

Lucy was, of course, greatly indignant and distressed, especially as she was feeling sick and dizzy and in no fit state to cope with disturbances. She would not hear a word against Nicholas, whom she excused by pointing out that he was grieving for the death of his brother and greatly hurt by the terms of his will.

'But it's all right if you are upset by the loss of Mattie,' I said.

'I'm sure he'll change his mind. He probably doesn't realize how much I depend on her. I'll talk to him about it.'

That, I felt sure, would achieve little.

In the afternoon I set out for Monkstone, hoping to meet William and tell him of the latest developments. Unfortunately he was not there and I was received in the drawing room by Helena, who was elegantly attired in a lavender moiré silk dress ornamented with black lace and ribbons. It was, I supposed, appropriate for an almost-fiancée. Full mourning hardly seemed correct whereas normal colours might suggest levity.

'I've no idea when William will be back; he's gone over to Bromsley on business. However, you'd be very welcome to stay for tea and we can have a nice chat.' Although she smiled I fancied the invitation had a frosty edge to it but I decided to stay in the hope William would soon return.

I told her what I intended to tell her brother: that I had been dismissed as governess and Mattie as Lucy's personal attendant.

'Ah, so he's decided on a school for Alice after all. That may be the best solution as the house is to be sold, but none of you must think of leaving yet. There is plenty of time; the will has to be sorted out first and then I must find a purchaser.'

'I don't care about myself,' I said. 'I only took on the employment as a temporary measure but I am concerned about poor old Mattie. She was in tears about it and she doesn't often cry.'

'It does seem harsh, certainly, but Nicholas Blackwood is like that. Once he gets an idea in his head nothing can shift him. He's utterly selfish and domineering. I've never liked him.

Poor Ambrose was worth ten of him.'

Any ally was useful. Helena might not want me to marry her brother but that did not mean she could not be a help to me in other ways.

'I have not trusted him since he married my sister,' I told her. I began to tell her a little of how our acquaintance began.

'He obviously married your sister for her money — as he did his first wife. Dear Lucy has many personal attractions but if she had not it would have made no difference. No doubt her delicate health was also an inducement. Do I sound cruel? I'm sorry, but it is no more than the truth. The first Mrs Blackwood was a plain, meek little mouse and strictly between ourselves I always thought there was something strange about her death.'

'I understand she died in childbirth,' I said, unwilling to repeat what Mattie had told me.

'Not quite. I was in Italy at the time, of course, but I had the whole story from William. I still have his letter; I thought it might be significant and kept it. Esther Blackwood gave birth to a female child which died a few days later but she seemed to be recovering. Then, a week later, she had a sudden relapse. It was marked by violent sickness which weakened her still further and after lingering on another week or two, she died. It never appeared a happy marriage to me. William thought she seemed afraid of Nicholas. She was too timid to stand up to him, I suppose.'

We sipped our tea together amicably enough and then she suddenly asked: 'Did you want to see William about some specific matter?'

'Not at all. It's such a pleasant afternoon I came out for a walk and I thought I might just as well come this way as any other. I was going to bring Alice with me but her father whisked her off on some other expedition — rather unusually as he never bothers with her much. I expect he wants to keep her as far away from me as possible.'

I took my leave shortly after this, rather disappointed that William had not returned but feeling better disposed towards his sister. On my return to Avalon Castle, however, the conversation with Helena was pushed out of my mind by more serious concerns. Lucy had taken a turn for the worse.

20

Dr Sawyer had been sent for. Lucy's symptoms had grown worse and Nicholas was raging about the house in a foul temper because the doctor did not arrive immediately. It transpired, when the good man did finally show up, that he had been visiting another patient two miles in the opposite direction. This seemed perfectly reasonable to me, anxious as I was, but Nicholas was incandescent. I thought his outbursts upset Lucy far more than a calm and comforting presence. She clutched my hand, moaning in pain and begging to see Mattie.

As Nicholas refused point-blank to leave the room, the doctor persuaded him to stand at a distance and maintain silence while he examined the patient. He alarmed us both by suggesting cholera but then decided that perhaps after all it was gastritis.

'We must wait and see,' he said solemnly. 'In the meantime, lead acetate and opium pills every two hours. I shall call again tomorrow morning.'

'That sounds rather drastic,' I said.

'But if it *is* cholera — ' Nicholas interposed.

'We'll know better tomorrow. Let her rest and sleep. Where is that old nurse who was here last time?'

'Left her employment,' said Nicholas shortly.

'But still in the house and anxious to help,' I added.

'Then send for her — the poor girl needs all the comfort we can give her.'

Nicholas agreed reluctantly, on the understanding that Mattie would only be allowed to attend Lucy for the duration of her illness.

Dr Sawyer came, as promised, the following morning. Lucy was no better.

'Gastritis,' he said, 'as severe an attack as I've seen. I will prescribe something to settle her stomach, consisting mainly of arrowroot and a tonic to give her some strength.'

Two bottles were placed on a tray at Lucy's bedside together with a glass and spoon. Opium pills, to help her sleep and to be used sparingly, were kept in a locked cupboard in the dressing room.

After several days Lucy seemed little better and Nicholas was obliged to return to town 'on matters of business'. Dr Sawyer had recommended a bland diet but Lucy ate very little and seemed to have lost her appetite completely. She began to look thin and wasted and her eyes were watery and red. Then she seemed to develop laryngitis and her voice grew hoarse so speaking became an effort and it was sometimes difficult to tell what she said. Mattie's honey and lemon remedy did not help at all.

Mattie became very worried and was further annoyed by the continual presence of Lizzie Fox, whom she always referred to as 'that spy'. When Lizzie was told to find occupation elsewhere she said Mr Blackwood had told her to stay with his wife at all times.

Nicholas returned at last and it was left to me to express doubts about Lucy's condition. 'She is no better — in fact I think she's worse. Dr Sawyer is a dear old man but doesn't seem to have any answer to the problem. He keeps saying it's gastritis but if so it has some very strange effects. Ought you not to call in a younger medical man who might have a more modern and energetic approach to diagnosis?'

'Nonsense! Sawyer is perfectly capable and very experienced. He's treated Ambrose and Jessica and me since we were children. If he says it's gastritis, then that's what it is. You are worrying needlessly. I knew no good would come of that old woman fussing around.'

Nicholas was certainly kind and gentle with Lucy, speaking softly and soothingly to her, stroking her face and hair. 'Acting the part of a concerned husband' was the thought that occurred to me.

While he was there he must have persuaded Lucy to make more effort because one day she declared she felt considerably better and would go downstairs to dinner. As she was very weak Nicholas carried her down himself and helped her to a seat at the dining table. After two spoonfuls of soup she said she felt sick and had to be taken back to her room.

I had noticed one odd thing about her attire. She wore one of her evening dresses which Mattie and Lizzie had helped her into, but there was a lace scarf round her neck and her hair was dressed lower than usual. I followed her to her room, where Nicholas was holding forth about the lack of proper care his wife was receiving.

I waited until he had gone and then helped Lucy undress. I carefully unwound the scarf and found an angry red rash on the side of her neck.

'How long have you had this?' I asked.

'A day or two,' she croaked.

'Dr Sawyer looked at it this morning and prescribed a salve but I'm going to try some of my sulphur and lard — it works wonders,' said Mattie.

I said no more but I was beginning to think that neither Mattie's homely remedies nor even Dr Sawyer's medicines were going to help Lucy. When her hair was taken down and Mattie brushed it gently it seemed to me that too many hairs were tangled in the bristles. Her hair had lost its lustre and seemed thin and lifeless.

During this time I saw William Norton rarely and for a few minutes only. He understood my anxiety and, like me, was doubtful of Dr Sawyer's ability.

'We used to call him Old Sawbones when I was a child and he seemed about ninety then. I imagine if Nicholas was ill himself he'd consult a younger man.'

'The trouble is, Nicholas is adamant that Dr Sawyer is perfectly competent. Lucy, of course, always agrees with him, but she likes the old man and he's certainly gentle and sympathetic.'

William looked troubled. 'If it was gastritis it should have improved by now.'

'Those medicines she's taking don't seem to have done much good but the worst thing is this lack of appetite. She's eating very little and that's making her worse.'

'Nicholas isn't here all the time. If it was

my sister I'd wait until he'd gone back and call in somebody else. Turner is considered the best doctor in Bromsley. He's in his early forties, so he's old enough to have some experience but young enough to be up to date and capable.'

'Is it the right thing to do — to employ one doctor and call in another behind his back?'

'Everyone is entitled to a second opinion. You could mention it to Dr Sawyer if you like. Confound his feelings! You shouldn't have to worry like this.'

He put his arms round me, which was a great comfort. I wished I could stay there forever but anxiety spoils every joy.

★ ★ ★

Once or twice Lucy seemed to rally. She managed to get out of bed and totter to her boudoir with a rather curious gait. 'I fear my muscles are wasting — I must use them now I am recovering.'

But as her illness continued into its third week any idea of recovery receded. Nicholas spent much more time at Avalon Castle so it became difficult to follow out William's plan. I suggested to him that we should consider sending for Dr Turner and Nicholas flared up into one of his rages.

'Turner? Why Turner? Who put that idea into your head, pray? I've heard of this Turner — a charlatan — an upstart — a quack! I'm not having him anywhere near Lucy with his bumptious, arrogant ways. If I found *anyone*' — he glared at me — 'had sent for Turner behind my back there would be the devil to pay.' He grinned unpleasantly. 'And don't forget the devil is Old Nick!'

21

To my great relief, a few days later Lucy began to show signs of improvement. She was still very weak but she said she felt better and had recovered her appetite. A little steamed fish and rice pudding were eaten with some degree of enjoyment and, best of all, no vomiting followed.

Dr Sawyer, who had attended her devotedly every day, pronounced her well on the road to recovery, but he seemed as surprised as I was.

Calf's-foot jelly, minced chicken breast, beef tea and gruel all followed in the next few days and she began to brighten visibly: her eyes cleared, her complexion improved and she began to recover some of her vitality. When she declared she was tired of her invalid diet Mattie hastened to provide her with more substantial food. Lucy still needed to rest and it was obvious she would require time to restore her to full health, but at last I ceased to worry about her.

Nicholas was staying in Birmingham to attend to business matters arising from Ambrose's death — or so he said. One weekend he returned and seemed rather irascible, greeting news of Lucy's improvement with a curious mixture of surprise and impatience.

'I told you Sawyer was a good doctor and you wouldn't believe me,' he said.

'Aren't you relieved?' I asked.

'Of course I am! I just hope there won't be a relapse, that's all.'

'Why should there be?'

'How do I know? Life is full of disappointments. Never hope for anything — then you won't be hurt.'

He showed some perfunctory pleasure when he visited Lucy and congratulated her on looking so much better.

'We'll soon have you up and about again. It's nice to see you sitting in a chair.'

'I can walk much more easily now and I manage to go to my boudoir every day for a few hours. I'm sure I'll be able to come downstairs soon.'

'Don't overdo it. Remember what happened last time.' He dropped a kiss on her forehead and left the room. On Monday morning he returned to town very early without saying goodbye to anyone. Lucy pretended not to mind.

A few days later there occurred an event which brought matters to a head.

On my return from a visit to the village I

overtook the postman and undertook to deliver the letters to the house. They were always placed on a tray in the entrance hall and the butler saw they were passed on to the recipients. I glanced at the names on the envelopes: one for me from Mrs Purcell, one for Jessica, three for Nicholas and one for Ambrose from someone who had not yet heard of the tragedy. Something made me look again at this last envelope. It bore a London postmark. I was about to put it on the tray when I was interrupted.

'I'd better have that!' said a gruff female voice and Jessica's hand stretched out to receive the letter addressed to her brother. She tore it open at once and read it on the spot. I was not at all sure if this was the right thing to do but it was hardly my concern.

'Strange business!' she said, and handed the letter back to me. 'You read it and tell me what you think. You seem to have some common sense and you're not involved with anything that's going on here.'

The letter bore the address of a school for young ladies in Chelsea.

*25*th *April 1868*

Dear Sir,
Forgive me for troubling you but I

hardly know where to turn for advice and information. My sister, Miss Maria Carr, has been working as governess to Miss Alice Blackwood at Avalon Castle for two years. During that time she has written to me at irregular intervals, usually once a month.

I have heard nothing from her since last December and after waiting seven weeks I wrote to her twice to enquire if anything was wrong. I received no reply. I then wrote to Mr Nicholas Blackwood. Again I received no reply.

I am now very anxious regarding my sister's whereabouts and well-being. As you are the brother of her employer and the owner of the house where she has been living, I wondered if you could possibly let me know what has happened to her and where I may find her. If she has left her employment I cannot understand why she has not let me know.

I await your reply with trepidation but will be ever grateful for your assistance.
    Yours faithfully
    Jane Carr

'This is strange,' I said. 'She left so suddenly and it was supposed she had gone to join her sister in London. It looks as though she never arrived.'

'Or never intended to go there — or even — ' Jessica chose her next words carefully, 'or even didn't get very far from here.'

'She left no letters and spoke to no one before she departed,' I said. 'Even Alice thought it was strange.'

'And no one saw her leave.'

'Except your brother, who took her to the station early in the morning.'

'Yes.' Jessica's mouth set in a grim, straight line.

'Perhaps if you show him the letter he will be able to tell you something.'

'Why should he? My brother he may be but he never confides in me. He's hardly aware of my existence. Ambrose was different.'

'I know he was — a complete gentleman.'

I thought she had softened a little towards me and it was obvious she had no great trust in or affection for her brother Nicholas.

'What are you going to do with the letter?' I asked, rather cautiously. I expected her to say, 'That's my business,' but she shook her head and put the envelope and its contents in her pocket.

'I'm not sure yet, but I may reply to it myself. Don't mention this to anybody, but if you find out anything, let me know.'

'Of course I will. Something is wrong, I feel it.'

'So do I!' She walked away from me without another word.

This incident left me restless and anxious. I remembered being puzzled about the removal of Miss Carr's trunk which, according to Alice, was a cheap wickerwork item covered with canvas. It would be light enough when empty but heavy when packed with books and clothes, even though she had left some of the former behind. She was a small woman and I could not imagine her dragging it down the steep backstairs by herself. Nicholas could have managed it, but why should he when he had dismissed the woman and she was in disgrace? Would he not have called up one or two of the menservants?

I decided to go up to the attic where I knew the luggage of the household was stored, trying to suppress the suspicion that Miss Carr's trunk might still be there. Joe Hicks had loaded it into the gig, but he had not actually seen Miss Carr on that occasion.

The attics lay on two sides of the third storey, the other sides being occupied by the servants' bedrooms. As the house was comparatively new these garrets were not as cluttered as one might expect; indeed, two were almost empty and a third contained rolled-up carpets, a croquet set, cricket bats and boxes of books. The last proved to be the one I was searching for. It was full of trunks, valises, bags and cases of the sort used by travellers. I found my own trunk, and Lucy's. Two others bore the initials AB and had obviously belonged to Ambrose. None answered the description I had been given of Miss Carr's trunk. I turned to go, obscurely disappointed, and then paused by the door. It would do no harm to look inside the boxes that were unlocked. They yielded nothing of interest until I came to Jessica's. Its owner was indicated by a label attached to one of the handles.

It was full of clothes. On top lay a familiar paisley shawl of red and purple, knotted together to make a bundle. When I untied it I found a brush and comb and all the contents of a woman's dressing table, hastily swept into the first wrapping that had come to hand. Among the smaller things were two glittering amethyst earrings. I could not believe Miss Carr had left these behind voluntarily.

I investigated further. Everything was badly packed as though carelessly flung inside. Books and writing materials were mixed up with the attire. There was a grey dress I recognized and several flimsy items of underwear and night attire made of very thin silk and obviously expensive. Not at all the sort of thing one might expect a governess to own. The items were enclosed in a bed sheet which had obviously been used to carry them upstairs.

Why were all Miss Carr's possessions in Jessica's trunk? Probably because it was the first to come to hand. I had a mental vision of Nicholas bundling up Miss Carr's possessions, hauling them up to the attic and throwing them into his sister's trunk. Then he went down to where the dead governess lay, wrapped in a sheet, and pushed her into her own trunk, which he dragged downstairs and let Joe Hicks heave into the gig.

I remembered the unlocked boathouse and *Golden Wings* drifting on the lake next morning. With a shudder of horror I realized how Miss Carr's body was probably disposed of. Nothing could be proved unless the lake was dragged and how could I persuade the authorities that it was necessary? It was essential to find out more.

When Nicholas was staying at Avalon Castle he had the use of a room next to the library as his study. This was known as the map room as a large collection of cartography was kept there, but there was also a bureau and a table where papers could be spread. I slipped in unobserved and found, as I had foreseen, that the flap and drawers of the bureau were all locked. I had brought with me a collection of keys from cupboards and pieces of furniture about the house. After trying them all in turn I found one that did the trick with a little help from a hairpin. I let down the flap of the bureau. The pigeonholes were full of papers which were of no use to me until I found two envelopes with London postmarks. I recognized the writing from the letter Jessica and I had read. A quick glance told me that they did indeed come from Miss Carr's sister. I put them back where I found them.

Next I investigated the small drawers and the tiny cupboard in the top of the desk. I found a small glass jar with no label, which contained bluish crystals. I dipped my finger in but they were quite tasteless as well as odourless. I found an empty envelope and tipped some of the substance inside.

Having now seen all I wanted I fastened everything securely again. I had carried out the task with very little sign of the lock being forced and I thought that if I went in again with a piece of walnut I could cover up the faint scratches I had made.

I was relieved to return to the library, even

though Nicholas was not in the house. I suppose I could always have said, if discovered, that I had been searching for a map to assist Alice in her studies. Although I had been dismissed as governess my pupil was so bored and listless that I still found her tasks to do when her father was not present.

Next I found the butler, who was engaged in polishing the silver. He seemed quite willing to chat for a few minutes and at once remembered finding the letters from London addressed to Miss Carr.

'Mr Nicholas was at home when the first arrived so I took it to him as he had been Miss Carr's employer. ''Ah yes,' he said. 'I will post this on to the lady in question. If other letters for her arrive then let me have them, even if you have to keep them until I come here. I know where they are to be sent.' Did I do the right thing, Miss Garland? It seemed all in order to me.'

'I'm sure it's nothing,' I said, unwilling to confide in him further. For all I knew he could report our conversation to Nicholas and if I asked him not to mention it, his suspicions would be aroused.

That afternoon I set out for Monkstone, anxious to consult both William and his sister. To my disappointment she was again sitting in the great bay window on her own, but she assured me that William had only gone outside for a few minutes and would soon be joining us.

'He won't be late for his favourite cake,' she smiled, and then looked at me closely.

'I can see you're upset about something,' she said. 'Is that why you've come to see us?'

'Yes, but I'd rather wait until your brother is here so I can tell you both.'

At that moment there was a tap on the window and William Norton stood outside, smiling broadly. Nero put his paws on the windowsill and made a steamy, slobbery patch on one of the panes.

'Do hurry and join us!' Helena cried. 'But no dirty boots — or paws!'

'I promise but I can't guarantee no smell — I've just come from the stables.'

As soon as he entered the room I could contain myself no longer.

'I have just done something quite appalling,' I said. 'Something positively criminal — and I have to admit I'm not in the least ashamed.'

I described how I had investigated the trunks in the attic following the arrival of the letter from Miss Carr's sister.

'But that's not criminal,' protested Helena. 'You had a perfect right to go to the attics.'

'It's what I feared might be there — Miss

Carr's trunk and — I don't know — but it wasn't there.'

'So you had your journey for nothing,' smiled William.

'Not exactly. All Miss Carr's clothes and possessions were crammed into a trunk belonging to Jessica Blackwood. Why did she take nothing with her? Not even a hairbrush or her earrings!'

'This sounds strange,' said William. 'But there's more, isn't there?'

'I managed to unlock Nicholas's bureau in the map room. The letters from Miss Carr's sister were bundled into one of the pigeonholes. I also found this . . . '

I produced the envelope containing the bluish crystals I had removed from the desk.

William frowned. 'Where did you find this?'

'There's a jar of it in an inner compartment. I poured a little into this envelope.'

'May I keep this? I'd like to take it to a chemist. It looks to me like arsenic.'

'I had a horrible feeling it might be but I thought arsenic was white?'

'So it is, but some years ago a law was made stipulating that arsenic, when sold to the public, must be coloured with soot or indigo. The purchaser must also sign the poison book. This means little. It could have been bought from a chemist in a large town such as Birmingham or Worcester. The purchaser is supposed to be known to the seller, but I'm sure that condition is not always observed. Anyway, arsenic is often bought for the poisoning of vermin and I believe some ladies use it as a whitener for their hands.'

'True,' said Helena, 'but I've never needed it.'

'Do you think what I did was wrong?' I addressed them both but it was William who answered.

'I'd probably have done the same in your place. Your first concern must be for your sister.'

'I must go back!' I suddenly felt cold with fear, remembering Nicholas talking of 'a relapse'. I think that if Lucy had not been at Avalon Castle I would never have set foot in it again. But I had to return and do all I could to protect her.

22

To my relief I found Lucy in her room, still looking far from well but on her feet rummaging through the clothes in her closet, throwing garments on the floor.

'I do wish Mattie could help me. I can never find anything. Now I'm so much better Nicholas has forbidden her to attend me. That stupid Lizzie is so slow. I'm sure she does it on purpose to annoy me. Dinner could well be over before I'm dressed. She knows it's time to get ready and she's not here. I don't know how the Other One put up with her. She's not a proper lady's maid at all but I get the impression that the Other One didn't care how she looked.'

Lucy rarely referred to her predecessor and never by name.

'What happened to all her things?' I asked.

'I don't know and I don't care. I believe Nicholas gave away all her clothes. He sent them to some charity.'

'But there must have been other items — toilet articles, a workbox, luggage, a jewel case, books — '

'I don't get the impression she did much

reading — just interminable Berlin wool work. Why are you so interested?'

'It's an idea I have. It may come to nothing and I can't really explain it yet because I don't know what I'm looking for.'

'Jessica might know, I suppose. I've never asked Nicholas about the Other One.'

As I had told Lucy, I was not at all sure what I expected to discover, but I wanted to find out more about Nicholas Blackwood's first wife; the quiet, mousy woman who had made so little impression that no one ever mentioned her. It was just as though she had never existed. She had no close relations, I seemed to recall, but had been orphaned early in life and had inherited a considerable fortune from her parents. She had been brought up by an aunt who had since died. The fortune had sunk to very little owing to bad investment and the failure of a bank. How fortunate for Nicholas that her life ended when it did, leaving him free to pursue a younger and richer replacement!

No doubt Jessica could tell me what I wanted to know, as Lucy had suggested, but I still felt uneasy about Miss Carr's possessions being in her trunk. This was probably nothing to do with her but she was so taciturn and difficult that I could not consider her entirely innocent without some sort of proof.

At that moment Lucy's maid Lizzie Fox entered the room, carrying a pile of linen.

'Everything washed and ironed, ma'am,' she announced, addressing Lucy. 'I'll help you change for dinner, since you're feeling so much better.'

'The blue dress, please, and you can put everything back in its place. Why don't you go and change, Rachel? There isn't much time.'

I indicated to Lizzie Fox that I wished to see her afterwards. I went to my room and changed as quickly as I could. It would cause surprise if I did not appear, especially as Lucy was going down, and as Nicholas was sure to be present I had no wish to rouse his suspicions. I hurried back in the direction of Lucy's room just in time to catch Lizzie leaving it.

'There's plenty of time after all, miss. I've persuaded Mrs Blackwood to have a rest before dinner.'

'Very wise,' I said, walking with her to the end of the passage. 'I understand you were Mrs Esther Blackwood's maid.'

'Not really — well, sort of. She had a maid but Mr Blackwood got rid of her and asked me to take over.'

'Got rid of her?'

She shrugged. 'Dismissed her. I don't know

why. Mrs Blackwood seemed quite satisfied with her.'

'So this has happened before?'

'Yes, I suppose so.'

'And when did this happen?'

'Before she had the baby — the one that died. There was old Dr Sawyer and a midwife but they couldn't save her or the child. They lingered on a few days and then it was all over.'

'Do you know what became of Mrs Blackwood's things?'

'What things, miss? Her clothes were all given away.'

'Not clothes. Small possessions — bits of furniture — a workbox, that sort of thing.'

'She had a little worktable, one of those with a bag underneath.'

'That's the sort of thing I had in mind. I understand she used to do Berlin wool work and I need some wool of an unusual colour. I wondered if she might have left some. Do you know what became of the worktable or any other furniture she might have used?'

'There was a writing desk, one of those that fold up like a box. I think that's in one of the bedrooms with the worktable. It was the one with the lilies painted on the bed.'

'Ah, I know the one you mean. Thank you, Lizzie. I'll go there now. It will save a trip to the haberdasher's if I can find what I'm looking for.'

At once I went to the bedroom with the lilies. All the rooms had romantic Arthurian names and this one was called Galahad. It was a comparatively small and austere apartment, sandwiched between Lancelot and Bedevere, and hung with dark-blue serge. The bedhead was painted with lilies and there was a tapestry of Sir Galahad kneeling before the Holy Grail.

In the small oriel window stood a mahogany worktable with a faded pink silk bag beneath. I went through it carefully but it contained nothing beyond the usual require-ments of a needlewoman: needles and thimbles, spools of thread, rolls of ribbon, a pincushion and a bundle of patterns. One of these bore a few words in a small neat hand.

There had been mention of a writing desk and there it was: a rectangular rosewood box with the initials E.W. engraved on the inlaid brass plate in the centre of the lid. Obviously this had belonged to Esther before her marriage.

It opened into a writing slope covered in red leather with a row of compartments for pens and inkwells. The two halves of the slope lifted to reveal neat packages of stationery and a prayer book inscribed: 'Esther Wing-field, for her seventh birthday.' That was all — no letters, no diary, no address book. But then, wouldn't Nicholas have destroyed such things? I was about to close the desk when I remembered that such pieces of furniture often contained secret drawers. I pulled each of the dividing partitions in turn; there was a click and a panel sprang away to reveal three tiny drawers with ivory knobs. The first contained a lock of hair wrapped in tissue, the second a piece of paper which I unfolded with a shaking hand, but it proved to be the bill for the desk. The third held a small daguerreotype of a severe-looking woman in a lace cap. The aunt who had cared for Esther?

Then I remembered I needed something to cover my excuse for searching the room so I returned to the work-table and pocketed a skein of olive-green wool. In doing so I disturbed the package of patterns which was loosely tied together and now fell apart. As I gathered everything up I noticed an unposted letter, addressed in the same hand that had written 'Extra blue wool needed' on the topmost pattern, but weaker, as though shaking.

The envelope was directed to a James Weston Esq. at a solicitors' office in Worcester. There was no stamp. I slipped it into my pocket and was about to leave the room when the door opened in front of me, revealing Lizzie Fox with a smirk on her face.

'Did you find what you wanted, Miss Garland?'

'Yes, thank you.' I flourished the green wool. 'I shall know where to come now. There's quite a selection.' I thought it a little odd that she had come after me. There was no reason at all for her to be anywhere near this room.

'Haven't you other duties?' I enquired. 'There is nothing for you to do here.'

'Just thought you might need some help, Miss Garland, and I wasn't sure you'd found the right place.'

'Very well; there was really no need. You may go.' I watched her walk away with an insolent gait, determined not to hurry.

I did not trust Lizzie Fox. She was Nicholas's creature and I had no doubt she reported back to him any circumstances out of the ordinary.

Back in my own room I opened the unsealed letter. The paper looked quite fresh, as though it had never been removed from its envelope. It bore the Avalon Castle address and was dated a week before the writer's death. The writing was shaky and straggling and looked like that of a sick old woman.

Dear Mr Weston,

Forgive me for troubling you with my anxieties but I do not know who else I can approach for help and advice. There is no one here I can trust and you were very kind to me when my aunt died.

I am very ill and grow weaker by the day. The doctor is old and deaf and attributes my sickness to the effects of childbirth but I know this is not so. My symptoms are quite different. My husband will not send for another physician and has dismissed my maid, forcing me to accept the attentions of a young woman whom I do not like or trust.

I hardly dare commit my suspicions to paper but I must confide in you before it is too late. I believe my husband is poisoning me. He cares nothing for me and now all my money has gone I have become an impediment.

Please come to see me. You are my last hope. I have nowhere else to turn and you helped me once before. Pray God you will not be too late.

Yours in desperation,
Esther Blackwood

I felt quite cold inside and yet, curiously, not surprised. How the letter came to be hidden in the bundle of patterns would never be known. It was probably intended as a temporary place of concealment until she could find a reliable person to post it for her. The chance never came. My darkest suspicions were confirmed and more than ever I feared for Lucy. This letter, I felt sure, should be handed to the police. Would it be enough to ensure an exhumation? Somewhere or other I had read that arsenic left traces in the human body for years after death. But perhaps that last letter from poor Esther would be dismissed as the ravings of a dying woman suffering from puerperal fever.

Yet there was arsenic in Nicholas's desk. I was now entirely convinced that the substance I had found was indeed poison and was being administered to my sister.

I decided to consult William Norton as soon as possible. He would know exactly what to do and the police would be more inclined to listen to him rather than me. Should I return to Monkstone immediately? Weary as I was, I was about to seize bonnet and shawl when I hesitated. It would soon be time for dinner and Nicholas Blackwood would be present. My absence might make him suspicious.

I decided to write a note to William Norton, begging him to meet me at the stile in Hayfield Lane where I had something very important to show him and needed his advice urgently. Then I went down to the stables and found Joe Hicks, the boy who had always seemed trustworthy and obliging, and held out the note.

'Joe, if you take this to Monkstone as fast as you can, I'm sure Mr Norton will give you another sixpence to make this up to a shilling.' I slipped a coin into his hand.

His face lit up. 'Oh, thank you, Miss Garland. I'll go as fast as I can.'

'To Mr Norton directly, mind. Don't leave it with anyone else.'

We were a silent, gloomy party that evening: Nicholas, who had arrived just before the meal, was in one of his scowling, taciturn moods. Jessica was equally reticent and Lucy looked pale and unhappy, although she managed, I noticed, to eat some of her soup and most of the fish course. Her husband glared at her balefully and remarked on her improved appetite.

'Nice to see you so much better,' he added, but his expression indicated otherwise.

It was difficult for me to eat normally, though I did my best as I had no wish to draw attention to myself. I have no idea what I consumed; everything tasted of sawdust and I felt the cold, inner sinking of fear. Once or twice I looked at Nicholas, calmly eating his dinner, and wondered if I had imagined everything. Was it really possible that I was sitting at a table with a murderer?

Outside, beyond the deep-set mullioned windows, the early summer evening glowed green and gold. It was like one of those scenes ancient artists used to put in their pictures behind a Madonna or a martyrdom: a glimpse of the outside world where everything was normal and bright and infinitely alluring.

Lucy tried to lighten the atmosphere with a few cheerful remarks but there was no response so she lapsed into silence as if aware that the effort hardly seemed worthwhile. Afterwards I sat in the drawing room for a while with Jessica and Lucy, drinking coffee and longing to get away.

'It's a beautiful evening,' I said at last. 'I think I'll go out for a walk before it gets dark. A breath of fresh air always makes one sleep better.'

There was a time when Lucy would have offered to come with me but she smiled faintly and said she was going to bed. I had no means of knowing exactly what time William Norton would be able to meet me. I had suggested half-past eight or later in my note, which would give him time to ride over from Monkstone but would allow for any delays. As far as I knew Helena and he were dining alone.

At a quarter past eight I put on my bonnet and shawl and gave the impression — for I did not know who might be watching — that I was going out for a leisurely stroll in the park. Once among the trees I quickened my pace and soon reached the stile in the wall, climbed over and sat to await William's arrival.

At first I enjoyed the peace of the quiet evening. The fresh green of the trees and hedgerows and the liquid song of a blackbird induced a feeling of calm. After a while my tranquillity began to fade. I glanced at my watch and found I had been waiting for only fifteen minutes. It had seemed much longer. I knew William would do his best not to keep me waiting but a request to see him at such short notice could not guarantee his arrival at half-past eight.

I grew increasingly uneasy. The sun had sunk low enough to give a slight gloom and it was growing chilly. My apprehension intensified and I walked a little way down the lane. I did not dare go too far: if he rode or came in the gig he would certainly come up the lane but if he walked he would emerge from the footpath a little way in the other direction.

At last I returned to the stile, huddled my shawl more closely round my shoulders and made a determined effort not to look at my watch. Presently I began to invent reasons why he was late, none of them at all unlikely yet none of them entirely convincing, for by now I felt sure something had gone wrong.

Then, in the growing dark, I heard a cheerful sound: a man whistling 'La donna è mobile'. I sprang to my feet, heart pounding, overwhelmed by relief and ready to throw myself into his arms. Where was he? I looked down the lane and then towards the spot where the footpath ended. As I heard no horse or vehicle he had obviously come on foot and that accounted for his lateness. Surely he couldn't now be teasing me when the situation was so serious?

'William!' I called.

The whistling resumed — just a few bars — and then silence. It is difficult to judge the direction of sounds but it seemed to me that this had come from somewhere behind me. I whirled round and saw nothing but the wall, the stile, overhanging trees and a ditch full of cow parsley, ghostly in the twilight. Suddenly everything seemed rather sinister.

I advanced a few steps in the direction of the footpath.

'William!' I called again, and then turned back.

'William!' a man's voice echoed mockingly, and Nicholas Blackwood stepped calmly over the stile.

'I'm afraid, my dear sister-in-law, that your admirer won't be coming here tonight. He didn't get your letter, but I did!'

23

Nicholas produced a piece of paper and shook it open. I recognized the note to William which I had handed over to the stable boy.

'I happened to arrive just as Joe Hicks ran out with this,' he said. 'I asked him a few pertinent questions and made him hand over your letter. It seems to me that you know a great deal too much. I'm also aware that my bureau has been searched: scratches round the lock, a few things a fraction out of place. I can guess what you found but I suspect there is more. You had better tell me at once exactly what you have discovered. It's obviously important enough to justify calling William Norton over here, and as you were at Monkstone this afternoon it must be something you have found out very recently.'

'I have no intention of telling you anything.'

'I'm sure you haven't and that's a very foolish attitude because it means I shall have to make you tell me. Between your return from Monkstone and writing the note to Norton you found some incriminating piece of evidence. Now, I understand you asked Lizzie Fox where my first wife's belongings were kept — '

'I always suspected she was your spy! No doubt that is why she was appointed as maid to my sister.'

'She directed you to the Galahad room and later saw you come out with a skein of wool. Come now, I can't believe that was all you found.'

'What else could there be? I don't know what you're talking about. If you'd kindly stand aside I'd like to return to the house.'

He smiled rather nastily but did not move.

'Well, I suppose I'd better go back another way as you're so ill-mannered.' I turned my back on him and began to walk briskly down the lane towards the main road where there was a better chance of seeing someone.

I heard the crunch of feet on gravel and started to run, but hampered by my skirts I was no match for a man and he caught me by the arm and twisted it painfully behind my back.

'Don't be stupid!' he growled. 'Do you want to be hurt?'

'Let go! How dare you!' I bleated foolishly, not expecting my words to have any effect. I was right — they didn't. I resolved to keep quiet as far as possible. If only someone

— anyone — would come along, but the lane was never a busy thoroughfare and at this time in the evening it was likely to remain deserted.

'You'd better come with me, Rachel, and I warn you, I carry a pistol and I'm quite prepared to use it if necessary. It is most unlikely that anyone will see us but I'd rather we moved from here to a less public place. You will climb back over the stile.' He pushed me forward, still holding my arm. For a few seconds he let go as I scrambled back into the park but when I reached the other side and wondered, briefly, what proportion of his threats were bluff, I suspected none. I glanced back and saw that he held a pistol.

'A revolver actually, of the latest design,' he said, seeing the direction of my gaze. 'It fires six bullets. This is just to convince you that it would be unwise to try and run away. I don't want to drag you along, so if you've any sense you'll walk quietly ahead of me and follow my directions.'

As I expected he told me to follow a path leading away from the house and I tried to guess where he might be taking me. The boathouse perhaps? The summerhouse? But we passed the pathway leading to both those places and still he urged me forward.

We came at last to the grotto, that rocky

artificial cave created in the last century by the owner of the old manor house. I glanced back at him enquiringly. He smiled grimly.

'Oh yes, we have arrived at our destination. I discovered many years ago that there is more to this antiquated construction than meets the eye.'

I peered at the grotto through the gloom, wondering why on earth I had been brought here. It was secluded enough, but hardly secure. He whistled — two or three piercing notes — and an elder bush moved. My astonishment grew as I saw that behind the bush was a small doorway and from it emerged Helena d'Ortoli.

For a moment my hopes rose, only to sink again as I realized how I had been deceived. She smiled at me.

'Oh dear, Rachel, what a nasty surprise for you! Come and see our little hideaway. We discovered it when we were not much more than children but no one else was ever aware of its existence. It's always been our secret.'

'Go in!' said Nicholas abruptly. 'There's a room behind the grotto. Not as uncomfortable as you might suppose.'

I found my legs were shaking — the result of fear and shock combined. I had to bend a little to enter the tiny doorway, brushing aside a mass of ivy that hung over the lintel. At the back of the grotto was a narrow room, no more than eight feet deep but a good eighteen feet across so that it ran almost the full width of the outer construction. It was lit by three tiny window slits screened outside by greenery and there was a small fireplace and several pieces of furniture including a bed, or rather a divan piled with cushions and rugs. It was very dim inside despite a small oil lamp flickering on a table.

The grotto was cut into the side of an artificial mound and the windows were almost level with the ground; even in full daylight little sun could penetrate the weeds and brambles that had grown outside.

Nicholas stood inside the door with his arms folded. 'Now, Rachel, I think the time has come for you to tell us what you know. Obviously you have uncovered something you consider important. According to your note,' here he again produced the letter I had hastily scribbled to William, and waved it before my eyes, 'you have something you wish to show him so I presume it's some sort of document. You had better hand it over.'

I began to protest that I had nothing but he pounced on me, seized my arms and held them behind me while Helena searched my pockets.

'Ah, here we are!' she cried triumphantly.

'Read it out,' he said, still holding me fast.

She held the letter close to the lamp and rapidly read out Esther Blackwood's last plea for help.

'And where did you find this?' he enquired.

'Among her embroidery patterns.' My voice was high and wavering and did not seem to belong to me.

'I never thought of that,' he said. 'Remiss of me! I went through all her belongings but never looked at those. She was a stupid woman but had occasional glimmerings of intelligence which I never suspected. Now you, Rachel, are the opposite. You are a clever woman who is sometimes stupid — or rather, naive. It was foolish of you to try and contact Norton. But then, you never suspected Helena and me of a liaison. Not surprising: I don't think anybody did. We were too careful. But now you've found us out so we must decide what is to be done with you.

'That letter of Esther's would never stand up in a court of law, of course; it would be dismissed as the demented ravings of a woman who was still suffering from the after-effects of childbirth and grief. However, taken in conjunction with other matters — '

'I've no doubt I can find some way of getting the arsenic from William,' said Helena, 'but that again means nothing on its own. Lots of people use arsenic for a variety of reasons.'

I tried to keep them talking, though I scarcely knew what was to be gained from a few extra minutes. No one in the world knew where I was or what danger I was in.

'So you never would have married Ambrose?' I asked Helena.

'Good heavens no! It was always Nicholas since I was fourteen. We discovered this place about then. But it suited my purpose well to encourage Ambrose's devotion from time to time. I was in London when I heard Nicholas had married. At that time I had no money so I was ineligible. Then I took myself off to Italy and found myself a husband. Not that I wasn't fond of Francesco, but I was not too pleased to hear Nicholas had married a second time without consulting me!'

'Well, it would never have suited us to marry,' he said.

'Not until now,' she smiled, 'because now I've inherited everything I'm quite a catch, aren't I? And you must be very kind to me or I might sell everything and go back to Italy with the proceeds. I have property there too, so I'm really rather well off. If anything happens to me the lot will go to William and you can hardly marry *him*!'

'One thing you've overlooked,' I said. 'I

made a copy of that letter and hid it before coming out.'

'Liar!' he laughed.

'It *could* be true,' said Helena. 'Where did you hide it?'

'Do you expect me to tell you?'

'Yes,' he gave my arm a twist, 'eventually.'

I had not told the truth of course but I wanted them to go. Left to myself I could try to recover my courage and look for a way of escape.

'I shall be missed,' I protested.

'You said you were going for a walk,' said Nicholas. 'Perhaps next morning at breakfast your absence will be noted and at last a search will be made. You may be found — or not. In either case it will appear that you met with a nasty accident.'

'Don't tell me you haven't worked out how to get rid of her?' cried Helena.

'Oh, I've one or two ideas but I'm not telling her what they are. Let it be a surprise.'

'Where's the copy of that letter?' she asked, tweaking a lock of my hair quite painfully.

'In my room, in the top drawer of my dressing table in the handkerchief sachet. It's in an envelope addressed to the police. In the covering note I've suggested they might investigate a certain trunk in the attic and drag the lake.'

'What?' This was obviously a shock to Nicholas.

'What's she talking about? What trunk? Why drag the lake?' enquired Helena suspiciously.

'I'll tell you about it later,' he said roughly, by now thoroughly disconcerted. It seemed that Helena knew nothing about the disappearance of Miss Carr.

'We'd better go and look,' said Helena, 'and I want an explanation. She can't get out of here if we lock her in. It will give us more time to decide what to do.'

'Won't William wonder where you are?' I asked.

'Oh, I went to bed early with an imaginary headache. We've got all night.'

They left me at last, locking the door behind them. I threw myself onto the bed and lay for some minutes trying to overcome the trembling which shook me from head to foot. Then I forced myself to take action. I must either get out of this place or draw attention to my plight before they returned.

I must have light! It was probably still twilight outside but in here it was quite dark. Helena had blown out the lamp so I began to search for some matches and at last found some in a window niche. That was careless of them, I thought. When I had lit the lamp I felt a little better and began to survey the room.

The windows were too narrow to squeeze through so I tried the door. Although old it was very solid with heavy iron hinges and a large lock. I thumped it a few times but it felt completely immovable. I next tried the fireplace but although reasonably wide it narrowed greatly towards the top. The walls were rough but solid. Beside the bed there was a small table, a chair and some shelves on the wall holding a few pieces of crockery, glasses and a half-empty bottle of wine.

I began to lose hope again. Then I came across a few ancient gardening implements in an alcove to one side of the fireplace. There was a rake, a hoe and a sickle, all very rusty, but the wood was sound enough and an idea was beginning to form in my mind.

As soon as I realized there was something I could do, my fear diminished and energy returned. I took sheets and blankets from the bed and with the aid of the sickle I tore them into strips. I then bound them firmly round the end of the hoe, taking care not to make it too bulky to go through the top of the chimney. I did the same with the rake. Then I lit a piece of candle I had found next to the matches before turning out the lamp; I used the oil to soak the primitive torches I had made. Going to the fireplace I lit the bundle of cloth at the end of the shaft and thrust the hoe up the chimney.

It flared up fiercely and I pushed the hoe as far up as it would go so that it would stand high above the chimney. I was not sure how well it could be seen: the grotto was surrounded by trees, mainly evergreens. There was, I recalled, a glimpse of the grotto to be had across the lake but I did not think it could be observed from the house. It might, however, be seen from the lane, though I had already found out to my cost how unfrequented it was likely to be at this time of day. It was impossible for me to see anything from indoors and I had to contend with bits of charred cloth and ashes dropping back down into the fireplace.

When the hoe seemed to be burnt out I used the rake in the same way, holding it by the toothed end, which I managed to wedge up the chimney so that I was free for a few minutes to see if there was anything else I could do. The door opened inwards so I pushed the table and chair against it, though these items were not heavy enough to provide a permanent obstacle. Still, if Nicholas was delayed for only a few seconds I might use that time to my advantage. I seized the wine bottle and stood behind the door.

He returned sooner than I expected. I

heard the rattle of the lock and the door burst open with enough violence to push the furniture some distance into the room. He kicked his way in and I brought down the bottle as hard as I could but the light was bad and he was moving so I succeeded only in striking a glancing blow on his shoulder. He staggered a little but did not lose his balance and whirled round to seize my wrist.

'No more tricks — understand?' I had heard of people 'snarling' and thought the expression melodramatic but no other word would do.

'I'm not going to let you, or anyone else, ruin everything at this stage.'

'If you saw the fire then others must have done so.'

'I shouldn't count on it. And by the time anyone arrives, you won't be here.'

I sank my teeth into his hand and he swore and released me, but he was between me and the door. As I backed away I heard a rattling clatter behind me. The rake had become dislodged and had fallen down the chimney. I seized it and held it before me. The torch end was burnt out but still smouldering and I pushed it towards his face.

He knocked it aside with his arm and took out his revolver.

'Even if I was a very bad shot, which I am

not, I couldn't fail to hit you at close quarters like this.'

Keep him talking, I thought — anything to gain time.

'How would you explain away my death?'

'Just a disappearance. Who cares if you don't come back? Lucy might snivel a bit but none of her feelings run very deep. And don't count on William Norton, that great amiable fool. Helena can make him believe anything.

'Now, you've wasted enough of my time. I suppose this stupid fire trick was an attempt to attract attention. It hasn't worked, I'm afraid. It's the lake for you, I think. If you are weighted down you should stay at the bottom for years.'

Suddenly something dark was flung across his throat and the arm holding the revolver was jerked in the air. There was an explosion and a fiery flash followed by smoke and an acrid smell. Somebody screamed and I realized it was myself.

24

Nicholas was struggling with another man — someone half a head taller than himself. There was much grunting and gasping but William Norton had the advantage of surprise as well as size. He managed to wrest the gun from Nicholas's grasp and then pushed him away.

'Now stand still or it might go off again and do you some damage. Rachel, are you all right?'

'Yes — thank God you've come!'

'I wouldn't trust him an inch. Is there something you can find to tie his hands?'

There were one or two strips of linen left from the shredded sheets and I had great pleasure in twisting and knotting them round Nicholas's wrists. We recovered Esther's letter, which William put away in his pocket.

'Copy indeed!' sneered Nicholas. 'I thought you were lying but I had to be sure.'

'Especially about the trunk in the attic,' I said.

'What's that?' enquired William.

'I'll tell you later. The police must be informed.'

'Well, we'll lock him in here until they arrive. Tie his ankles too to be on the safe side.'

We left him securely trussed, blew out the candle and removed the matches. Then we locked the door behind us and I threw myself into William's arms.

'How did you know?' I asked at last. 'He intercepted my letter to you.'

'Joe Hicks came to see me and told me you'd entrusted him with a note that his master had forcibly removed from his keeping. I found Helena had gone from her room and I at once suspected something was amiss. I know what she's like, better than anyone.'

We began to walk back to the house, his arm comfortingly round my waist.

'Helena never realized I suspected her of an affair with Nicholas,' he continued. 'I found out about it years ago and never trusted her since. She's my sister and I still love her for all her faults but she's always been flighty and selfish and capable of malice but I don't think she'd ever have done anything *really* bad if it wasn't for Nicholas. When I got here I saw him heading for the grotto and I guessed he was up to no good. I wasn't sure who was making the fire signal but I supposed it must be you. So I followed him. Rachel, are you sure you're all right? Can you go on?'

I had suddenly begun to shake and he tightened his arms about me.

'My poor girl! I shall have great pleasure seeing him pay for what he's done.'

'I'm not hurt, just frightened. I realize how close I came to dying. Let's go in. I shan't feel safe until we get to the house.'

The moon had risen, almost at the full, and its ghostly light added to the feeling of unreality.

'Where's Helena?' I said. 'They were going to search my room for a copy of Esther Blackwood's letter. Nicholas didn't really believe me but I don't suppose they could risk its being true. They must have thought they'd have the rest of the night to dispose of me. Nicholas planned to shoot me and throw me in the lake. Helena must have gone on alone after he turned back. It won't have taken her long to discover she's been duped.'

'I had some idea of attacking him before he reached the grotto but as I had no key and it might have been difficult holding him down and searching him in the dark, I thought it best to take him by surprise after he'd opened the door. I'd no idea he'd got a pistol or I might have had second thoughts.'

We reached the house at last and entered

by the garden door opening onto the passage leading to the main staircase. Coming down the stairs was Helena. She stopped when she saw us. An expression of shock was replaced by a faint smile. Even in such a situation I had to admire her self-possession as she continued her graceful descent of the stairs.

'You both have more intelligence than I gave you credit for,' she said.

'Do you really think I've trusted you all these years?' said William, stepping forward to block her progress. 'You always lied as a child if it meant you could get your own way or avoid a punishment.'

'And where has honesty got you, William? A shabby squire in a shabby old house with dog hairs on the furniture. I've always desired more than that. Whatever happens to me I've done what I wanted.'

'At other people's expense.'

'I presume you rescued Rachel here. Quite a modern Saint George, though she's scarcely a princess. Nicholas will be annoyed when he finds the bird has flown. He saw the fire from the porch and turned back to find out what was going on. I went up to search Rachel's room — needlessly of course. Did you see him?'

'Yes, and he was rather put out,' said William.

'What do you mean?'

'When I arrived I saw the beacon and went to investigate. I followed him to the grotto and overpowered him. Now he's prisoner and I have to decide what to do with you.'

For the first time she showed fear. 'You're not going to hand me over to the police. I've not done anything wrong. I'm your sister, for God's sake!'

'Which is my misfortune. As to not doing anything wrong, I've no doubt a case could be made against you as an accessory.'

'But think of the disgrace to our family!'

'Not to me, but to you. Perhaps you should have thought of this before.'

'Why not let me go back to Italy? I'll never trouble you again. I have friends there and a house in Venice. If the worst comes to the worst I can always marry that disgusting old Cantarini. He's amazingly rich and likely to die before too long.'

'Perhaps that's punishment enough — if he manages to live another ten years. You must renounce your legacy from Ambrose. I'm sure you know his death was no accident.'

'Impossible to prove but you can have this frightful place with pleasure — you're welcome to it.'

'Oh, for God's sake, Helena, go! If ever we meet again I hope it won't be until we're too old to care any more.'

She smiled faintly and kissed him on the cheek. As she passed me she murmured: 'I suppose you'll marry him. You are just the sort of dreary wife I always suspected he might find. He has no taste at all.'

'I think my taste is excellent,' he said, taking me in his arms, 'and I hardly think Helena has room to talk.'

'What will she do?'

'Go back to Monkstone to pack and collect her Italian maid. Then they'll go to Bromsley and take a train for London. No doubt they'll end up back in Venice. I don't care what Helena does as long as she keeps away from us.'

'And what are you going to do now?' I asked a few moments later, reluctant to move my head from his shoulder but unable to rest while Nicholas still lay imprisoned in the grotto.

'I'm going to ride over to Bromsley to see if I can contact Inspector Carver. The police need to be informed as soon as possible.'

'Take me with you,' I begged, even though I realized my plea was both foolish and selfish.

'I can't, my dear. One travels faster than two. Besides it would be too much of a strain — you are still having fits of trembling. You'd better break the news to your sister. She's going to need your care.'

When he had gone I felt as though a support had been taken away. I thought I needed company so I made my way to the drawing room but I found it empty. The great hall and the library were also vacant but one of the servants told me that Mrs Blackwood was in her room. She gave me a strange look and when I caught sight of myself in a glass I saw why: I was wildly dishevelled and far from clean, my face smudged with soot, ashes and tears. I went to my room and washed and tidied myself. The process was familiar and soothing and I needed time to collect my thoughts.

At last I went to see Lucy and found her in her dressing gown, having her hair brushed by her maid Lizzie. Like Mattie, I now thought of the girl as 'that spy' and I would enjoy seeing her demoted. I sent her away and she departed with the pert smile I had come to expect.

When Lucy and I were alone I warned her to prepare herself for bad news. Her reaction when I began to explain what had happened horrified me. She refused to believe me and the more I tried to convince her, making every effort to remain calm and quiet, the more hysterical she became.

'It's all nonsense! You're making it up.'

'Why should I do that?'

'You've always been jealous. You wanted Nicholas for yourself.'

'That is very cruel, Lucy, but you are not yourself. Your health is not as it was.'

'I've always been delicate.'

'You've never had stomach trouble in your life.'

'I haven't got it now. I haven't been sick for ages and Dr Sawyer says I'm on the mend. I'm feeling much better — that's why I came down to dinner.'

'We were all very worried about you — I'm sure you were near death at one point. It would suit Nicholas very well if you did die so he could marry Helena. They've been lovers for years, ever since she was in her teens, and now she's inherited this place she's quite a catch.'

'You're mad — both you and that idiot William Norton. I must find out what you've done to poor Nicholas.'

'He's perfectly safe in the grotto but he must be left there until the police arrive.'

'I've never heard anything so stupid. They'll just laugh at you.'

She shook off my restraining hand, snatched up a shawl and ran along the landing and down the stairs, her weakness forgotten.

Love, I thought as I followed her, really is blind! At least it was, as far as my sister was concerned. Her way of dealing with problems was to hope they would go away so that everything would be as she wished. She was so besotted with her husband that she could see no fault in him. I was comforted by the thought that she had no means of releasing Nicholas from his prison as William had taken the key with him.

'You'll catch cold,' I told her when I caught up with her. 'Why don't you come back and dress properly?'

'I don't care — though if I did get a chill I suppose you'd say it was *his* fault.'

I followed her out of the house and through the moonlit park. Now I wished I had not told her where we had left him, but as my pleas and protests had failed I fell silent. Her foolishness had to be indulged and I could only hope she would calm down enough to listen to reason. If not, perhaps weariness and cold would exhaust her so that I could persuade her to return to the house.

It was dark among the trees and she was wearing only light slippers on her feet. She slipped and fell but she shook off my helping hand.

'I'm not hurt!' she snapped.

When we reached the grotto she stood, uncertainly. 'There *is* a door!' she exclaimed. 'I've never noticed it before. But it's not locked, it's open.'

She was right. The small door stood slightly ajar and a faint glimmer of light showed through the crack. I felt a pang of fear. In a few seconds several explanations occurred to me but none of them made sense. William was still on his way to Bromsley. Nicholas could not have escaped without help. And then I realized what had happened and I cursed myself for a fool. Of course: Helena had her own key to the grotto. When William and I had confronted her she had retreated remarkably quickly in the circumstances; she had been willing to promise anything in order to escape.

'Be careful!' I cried, plunging after Lucy, but she was inside before I could stop her. I heard her give a small gasp of bewilderment.

The room was as I had left it apart from the guttering candle-end still burning in its tin holder on the table; I had blown that out myself. On the floor lay the strips of linen I had used to bind Nicholas.

'I knew you'd made it up,' cried Lucy triumphantly.

'He's escaped,' I said. 'Helena must have come down here and let him out. They've probably gone off together. We'd better return to the house.'

I was now quite frightened. I had no idea where Nicholas was and even without firearms — and he must have access to a whole armoury of them — he was extremely dangerous.

'I don't mean you made it all up maliciously,' said Lucy, looking a little shamefaced now. 'I only meant you misinterpreted some perfectly innocent words and actions. After Ambrose's death we've all been on edge and I know Nicholas can seem rather brusque and eccentric at times. It's just his way and there's no harm in it. What's of consequence in a letter from a sick woman, full of fancies? And as for Helena — they've known each other since childhood almost and perhaps when they were very young there was some silly infatuation but that's all in the past.'

'Lucy,' I said wearily, 'he held a revolver and threatened to shoot me.'

'I'm sure he didn't mean it seriously.'

'Look around you. This is where he and Helena used to meet. There's a *bed*, for heaven's sake!'

'That's probably been there for many years.'

'But the bedding is quite new. Oh, is it you

really don't understand or you don't *want* to understand?'

I had said nothing to her about the disappearance of Miss Carr and decided not to mention it now. Perhaps, when the police dragged the lake, she might at last accept the truth.

'Come along, we must go,' I said. 'Do you feel well enough to walk back?'

'Of course I do — ' Her words ended in a shriek as she saw someone standing behind me in the doorway.

I whirled round, heart in mouth, and was greatly relieved to see Mattie.

'I followed you down,' she gasped. 'I'm all out of breath but I couldn't let you come here on your own. Miss Lucy, you must be worn out. You haven't walked as far as this in weeks.'

'I've done well, haven't I? Didn't I say I was much better?'

'No thanks to a certain person,' said Mattie, taking firm hold of Lucy round the waist. 'Now I'm going to help you along and you lean on me if you feel tired. Miss Rachel, you walk the other side and we'll get her back to her nice warm bed and I'll bring her a glass of milk. I don't think we need bother with that nasty Lizzie Fox any more.'

I think Lucy was almost relieved to find

Mattie taking charge as she did when she was a child. But more was to come.

'I never thought much of that Dr Sawyer,' Mattie declared. 'He was too old and fifty years out of date. Those two bottles of medicine for instance. They weren't doing you any good at all. In fact, I noticed you were worse after taking a dose. Anyone would think there was something in the bottles that shouldn't have been there. So I took it upon myself to change the contents.'

'Mattie,' I said, 'did you suspect — ?'

'What I might or might not have suspected is neither here nor there,' she replied, with studied vagueness. 'The white stuff I replaced with arrowroot. No harm in that and it's good for settling the stomach.'

'But it *was* mainly arrowroot,' Lucy protested.

'Mainly perhaps, but it's the part that wasn't arrowroot that concerned me. As for that nasty brown medicine: I made a mixture of ingredients that looked and tasted much the same. Cold tea, for a start.'

'Ugh!' cried Lucy. 'You could have poisoned me.'

'She doesn't understand yet, Miss Rachel, does she?' said Mattie.

'No,' I replied, 'but she will before long, I hope.'

236

25

Jessica was waiting for us on our return, demanding to know what was going on. I explained everything to her as quickly as I could, while Mattie conducted Lucy, now in a state of collapse, up to her room.

Jessica's face scarcely changed. 'There's bad blood in the family,' she said, 'and it comes out from time to time. We had an uncle who went to the bad but he took to drink and gambling. Nicholas was always up to mischief, even as a boy — wild and fiery; not like poor Ambrose, who was a saint compared with him. But I never thought it would come to this.'

'Well, he's gone off with the Contessa and I don't suppose we'll see either of them again.'

'Good riddance! And I hate to say it of my brother. And she's no better. A painted harlot!'

There was an interminable wait for William's return with the police. The local magistrate preceded them but he was unwilling to proceed with any investigation until they arrived so he was conducted to the library and provided with a plate of sandwiches and a decanter of wine.

They all appeared at last: William Norton accompanied by Inspector Carver, a police sergeant and a constable. After a hasty greeting William declared that he was going straight home to Monkstone with the sergeant to see if they could find any clues to the flight of the guilty pair.

In the meantime I was interviewed by Inspector Carver, who had already heard an account of the evening's misdeeds from William but wanted a description of events from my own lips.

Wearily I went through my narrative, interrupted occasionally by the Inspector's questions.

'He threatened to kill you?'

'Oh yes. He had a revolver and I've no doubt he was prepared to use it. He said he'd throw my body into the lake.'

'And you believe he was trying to poison his wife — your sister?'

'I'm sure of it. Dr Sawyer insisted she was suffering from gastritis but our old nurse was suspicious of the medicines he prescribed and replaced them with concoctions of her own, after which my sister's health began to improve. I believe poison had been added to the medicines. I've told you about the arsenic in Mr Blackwood's bureau.'

'Yes, but that could have been bought for any number of innocent reasons. It's difficult to bring a prosecution for poisoning if there is no clear evidence linking the purchase of poison with its administration. Did this nurse of yours preserve any of the medicine you suspect of being tampered with?'

'I doubt it, but you must ask her.'

'Ah, a great deal depends on that. The Marsh test can be used to extract arsenic from almost any liquid but if that liquid has been destroyed . . . ' He shook his head.

'There is something else — very important.' I told him about my suspicions concerning the disappearance of Miss Carr and the discovery of her possessions in a trunk in the attic.

'No one actually saw her leave,' I said, 'but the fact a boat was found floating on the lake next morning after her supposed departure may point to where she might be found.'

'We'll investigate first thing in the morning,' he assured me.

'And there's the death of Nicholas Blackwood's first wife. I have the last letter she wrote to her solicitor, begging for help. She was sure she was being poisoned.'

'Ah, that's a different matter. It would be difficult to prove anything after this length of time and with unreliable evidence, but I'll bear it in mind. We'd better concentrate on more immediate matters.'

He interviewed Mattie and Joe Hicks, and then attempted to question Lucy but was greeted with floods of tears and indignant reproofs from the protective Mattie.

At this point William returned from Monkstone with the news that the errant couple had got away. As the gig was missing he assumed they had driven to Bromsley to find a train.

'As soon as I got home I realized what had happened. Everywhere was in chaos. Helena had thrown a few clothes into a bag together with all her jewellery and Nicholas helped himself to some items from my wardrobe, my shaving tackle and my old boat cloak. He broke into my desk and took what money was there — about twenty pounds — and left everything in such a mess that I don't yet know what else he took.

'That Italian maid Helena brought with her was throwing hysterics on a grand scale. '*Abbandonata!*' she kept wailing, and that was all I could get out of her at first. Apparently, she was told to pack the rest of Helena's things and follow on as soon as she received word. I presume they are heading for Italy.'

'Would it be possible to stop them?'

'I've discussed this with Inspector Carver.

We can send telegrams to all the ports and railway stations but it will take time and they can still slip through. They could even hire a boat privately to take them across the Channel. Besides, the Inspector has to establish a crime has been committed by the two of them.'

The telegrams were despatched that evening and the railway staff at Bromsley interviewed but no further reliable information was forthcoming. One of the railway porters thought he had seen a man and a woman answering to the police description boarding the train for Birmingham but it was dark and there was a great deal of steam and other passengers milling about. From Birmingham, of course, they could have gone anywhere and despite enquiries, no one claimed to have seen them.

It wasn't until the next morning that more evidence came to light. Firstly, the trunk in the attic was inspected and its contents identified as those of the missing governess. I pointed out to the Inspector that this would have remained undisturbed had I not gone up to investigate. Nicholas would have had ample opportunity to dispose of Miss Carr's belongings when he eventually moved house.

The letters from her sister were still in Nicholas's desk, although he had got rid of the jar of bluish crystals.

Inspector Carver decided that there was enough indication of a crime to justify dragging the lake. Everyone kept out of the way except Jessica, who stood on the bank and watched the proceedings through opera glasses.

Apparently Miss Carr's flimsy trunk had broken apart and soon disgorged its gruesome contents, which were hauled up into the boat and covered with a tarpaulin.

'The young constable was sick over the side,' reported Jessica with a superior smile. 'The younger generation have no stamina.'

Inspector Carver sent word to the local coroner and called in the services of the doctors who usually performed post-mortems on those who died in mysterious circumstances. The results were communicated to us before the inquest among a welter of medical terms such as 'hyoid bone' and 'adipocere'. Miss Carr had died of manual strangulation. The verdict was 'murder by person or persons unknown'. The circumstances pointed directly to Nicholas Blackwood but the Inspector explained that the evidence was not enough to obtain a conviction.

'If he was back here in England we might try,' he added. 'But as to the other matter, there is no proof at all that he administered poison in your sister's medicine. Mr Norton, I understand, does not want the Contessa d'Ortoli charged with aiding and abetting. But apart from the assault and threats to you, Miss Garland, we have little to depend on. Mrs Blackwood, I'm sorry to say, is most uncooperative.'

This last fact I knew. Lucy wept a great deal but said nothing that might incriminate her husband. This made little difference at the time for we heard nothing of Helena or Nicholas for nearly three months. It was as though they had vanished off the face of the earth. All enquiries failed and we began to wonder if they had met with a fatal accident.

Then we received a letter from Helena, who was back in her Venetian palazzo. She told us that on leaving Monkstone in such extraordinary circumstances they had taken the train for Birmingham as we supposed, but instead of heading for one of the Channel ports they had journeyed to Holyhead. There they had boarded the ferry for Kingstown and had remained in Ireland incognito, living on the money and jewels they had taken with them.

When they surmised that the hue and cry had died down, by which time they had nearly died of boredom, they travelled to the Continent and to Venice. Helena's final words to William were, as I suspected, designed to produce an impression of contrition before making her escape. She had no intention of parting with any money or property that was due to her. Avalon Castle became hers and was at once put up for sale. It was necessary for her to open up a correspondence with her brother and Jessica about the disposal of the property and she generously let them keep a percentage of the proceeds to cover their trouble and expenses.

William and I were married three months after the departure of Nicholas and Helena. After a short honeymoon we settled happily together at Monkstone and invited Lucy to join us there as she had no home. She seemed quite glad to accept our offer, especially as she had Mattie in attendance.

William suggested to Lucy, after an interval, that according to the new divorce laws she could probably obtain a legal dissolution of her marriage owing to her husband's cruelty and desertion. She refused to consider it. Whether she thought he might come back to her, which was most unlikely, or that he might send for her to join him in Italy, there was no point in trying to convince her otherwise. I thought this was probably just as well. However, Lucy's freedom came later, in another way.

Alice was packed off to boarding school after many tears and protestations. She declared she wanted to stay at home with me as her governess. This was before Avalon Castle was sold.

'But this isn't your home now, Alice. We all have to leave because the house belongs to the Contessa d'Ortoli and she is selling it.'

'You can still be my governess somewhere else.'

'I'm afraid not. You see, I am going to be married.'

She considered the matter as though it was the most unlikely outcome imaginable.

'Who are you marrying?'

'Can't you guess?'

'Not old Dr Sawyer?'

'Of course not. It's Mr Norton.'

'Oh yes,' she conceded reluctantly, 'he's nice and I do love his dog.'

'But you'll be able to come and stay with us at Monkstone when you are home from school. You'll only be at Worcester, after all.'

She cheered up at that, especially when she considered the alternative, which was staying with her Aunt Jessica. At first she was unhappy at school and wrote complaining letters, but then she began to make friends and settled down at last, as happy as she would ever be.

I thought Nicholas must have been missing his old life, despite the pleasures of Venice. The joys of carnival, masquerade, opera and ball were not to his taste, though they suited Helena very well. William showed me her letters and I gained the distinct impression that Nicholas had started to sulk and become withdrawn and sullen.

'He scarcely speaks to me these days,' she wrote, about a year after their headlong departure from England. 'He refuses to join in the amusements which provide so much delight to everyone here. The beauty and history of the city mean nothing to him and he falls asleep at the opera. He does not relish his role as a *cavalier servente* and refuses to learn Italian. In short, he is growing quite tiresome.'

'What is a *cavalier servente*?' I asked William. 'Does it mean lover?'

'Well, it can mean that but it's rather more. The term is commonly used in Italy, especially in Venice, for a lady's gentleman attendant. He carries her gloves and shawl, summons a gondola when she needs one and generally makes life easier for her.'

'Nicholas must hate every minute of it — I hope!'

William grinned. 'I must say they deserve each other.'

By that time we had all left the house. Jessica, who had no wish to inhabit the cottage left to her by Ambrose, moved initially to Nicholas's small house in Birmingham to keep an eye on the family business. She was sent regular instructions on what to do, and although she did her best with the help of the manager, she grew weary of the task and wrote telling Nicholas so in no uncertain terms.

After just over a year in Italy we learnt that Nicholas had died of cholera during an epidemic. It struck me as ironic that he must have suffered the same initial symptoms he had imposed on poor Lucy. Helena seemed less than heartbroken and indeed, a few months later married the old Prince Cantarini, who had been pursuing her for years.

Jessica then decided to sell the business which had now reverted entirely to her, and moved to a small but comfortable house next to the Methodist chapel in Bromsley.

News of her father's death seemed to make little impression on Alice. After all, I reflected, she never had much to do with him and saw him only at weekends for an hour or two if he could find the time to notice her.

Jessica was now her guardian and discharged her duties faithfully but without much affection. She did not like children in general and Alice in particular.

'That child has bad blood, the same as her father,' she declared, 'and one day it will out!'

'She's a little odd because she's been neglected and her mother's death was a great blow to her. But I see no harm in her and possibly a great deal of good,' I assured her.

Jessica shook her head. 'We must wait and see.'

Lucy now had to face the truth about her husband, though she never mentioned him if she could help it. For a week or two after the grim news came from Venice she was very subdued but I was too occupied with other matters by then to give her my full attention.

'Justice has caught up with Nicholas at last,' said William. 'Helena will soon get over it. I don't think they were too happy when they actually had to live together. Clandestine meetings are much more exciting: they add fuel to the bonfire. A steadily burning stove does not appeal to the romantic spirit.'

'Do you think he could have been hanged if he'd stayed here?'

'Who can tell? A good barrister would probably have enabled him to wriggle out of it. Much of the evidence was circumstantial, after all.'

'He'd not have made a good impression in

the dock; he was too belligerent and arrogant.'

'Well, he's gone now, so there's no point speculating. At least poor Lucy is free at last. Let's hope she'll find some contentment in life.'

What remained of Nicholas's fortune, apart from his share of the business, reverted to Lucy and provided her with an adequate but modest income of three hundred pounds a year. This was a far cry from what she had received before marriage but she seemed to accept her reduced state with equanimity.

Our first son was born shortly before we heard of Nicholas's death and I was too much occupied with young James to give Lucy my full attention.

'I think you almost regarded Lucy as your child,' said William, with some perception. 'But she'll have to accept the fact that she's now a grown-up woman and a widow.'

Mattie had at once taken over as nursemaid and her attentions to Lucy were now only partial. It was then Lucy accepted William's offer of a cottage in the grounds of Monkstone Hall where she could be near to us but maintain some independence. She took on a couple of maids and Mattie looked in on her every day and promised to come at once if Lucy was ill.

Lucy looked pale and wan in her deep mourning but actually her health had improved considerably and she began to recover her old cheerful spirit.

As for William and me, we settled into being the most comfortable married couple imaginable in our shabby old house with our children, our dogs and each other. If we became the steadily burning stove of William's metaphor, we did not lack the occasional bonfire.

The house and estate were eventually bought, after a year's delay, by a rich manufacturer from the Black Country who was looking for an imposing country residence to impress his friends and enemies.

Our new neighbours considered us snobbish and unfriendly, though we greeted them pleasantly enough every time we had an encounter. There was a reason for this which we did not think they would understand. We were both determined never again to set foot in Avalon Castle.